Anna Gavalda is one of the most acclaimed authors writing in French. Her books are published in over thirty languages and include: *I Wish Someone Were Waiting For Me Somewhere*, *Someone I Loved*, *Hunting and Gathering* and *Consolation*.

Alison Anderson has translated many books into English and is herself a published novelist.

Breaking Away

GALLIC

Breaking Away

Anna Gavalda

*Translated from the French
by Alison Anderson*

Gallic Books
London

A Gallic Book

First published in France as *L'Échappée belle by* le dilettante
Copyright © le dilettante 2009

English translation copyright © Europa Editions 2011

First published in Great Britain by
Gallic Books, 134 Lots Road, London, SW10 0RJ

A CIP record for this book is available from the British Library

Hardback ISBN 978-1-906040-40-6
Paperback ISBN 978-1-908313-01-0

Typeset in Fournier MT by Gallic Books
Printed and bound by CPI Group (UK) Ltd, Croydon, CR0 4YY

2 4 6 8 10 9 7 5 3

I hadn't even sat down yet, one buttock still hovering, my hand on the car door, and already my sister-in-law was on the attack.

'At last! Didn't you hear us hooting? We've been waiting here for ten minutes!'

'Good morning,' I replied.

My brother turned round. A little wink.

'You okay, sweetie?'

'I'm good.'

'You want me to put your things in the boot?'

'No, thanks. All I have is this little bag, and my dress. I'll stick it on the back shelf.'

'Is that your dress?' she asked, raising an eyebrow at the ball of chiffon on my lap.

'Yes.'

'What … what is it?'

'A sari.'

'I see.'

'No, you don't see,' I corrected her gently, 'you'll see when I put it on.'

She pulled a little face.

'Can we get going?' asked my brother.

'Yes. I mean, no. Can you stop off at the corner shop, there's something I need to get.'

My sister-in-law sighed.

'Now what do you need?'

'Some hair-removal cream.'

'And you get that at the corner shop?'

'Oh, I get everything from Rashid! Absolutely everything!'

She didn't believe me.

'Are you ready? Can we go?'

'Yes.'

'Aren't you going to fasten your seatbelt?'

'No.'

'Why don't you fasten it?'

'Claustrophobia,' I replied.

And before she could start going on about failed skin grafts and the horrors of public hospitals, I added, 'Besides, I want to sleep a little. I'm exhausted.'

My brother smiled.

'Have you just got up?'

'I never went to bed,' I explained, yawning.

Which was a patent lie, of course. I had slept for a few hours. But I said it to annoy my sister-in-law. And I was right on target, bingo. That's what I like about her: I'm always right on target.

'Where were you this time?' she asked predictably, raising her eyes to heaven.

'At home.'

'You were partying?'

'No, I was playing cards.'

'Playing cards!'

'Yes. Poker.'

She shook her head. Not too hard, though. Wouldn't want to mess up that blow-dry.

'How much did you lose?' asked my brother, amused.

'Nothing. This time I won.'

Deafening silence.

'Might we ask how much?' she relented, adjusting her designer shades.

'Three thousand.'

'Three thousand! Three thousand what?'

'Well … euros,' I said, acting naïve. 'Roubles wouldn't be much use, now, would they?'

I chuckled as I curled up. I had just given my little Carine something to mull over for the rest of the trip.

I could hear the cogs turning in her brain: three thousand euros … click click click click … How many dry shampoos and aspirin tablets would she have to sell to earn three thousand euros? … click click click click … Not to mention employee benefits, and business tax, and local taxes, and her lease, subtract the VAT … How many times did she have to put on her white coat to earn three thousand euros, net? And the Social Security? … add eight, take away two … and paid holiday … makes ten, multiply by three … click click click …

Yes. I was chuckling. Lulled by the purr of their saloon car, my nose buried in the crook of my arm, legs tucked up under my chin, I was pretty proud of myself, because my sister-in-law, she's a piece of work.

My sister-in-law Carine studied pharmacy, but she'd rather you said *medicine*, so she's a pharmacist, and she has a chemist's shop, but she'd rather you said *pharmacy*.

She likes to complain about her bookkeeping just when it's time for dessert, and she wears a white coat buttoned up to her chin with a thermal adhesive label that has her name stitched between two blue medical logos. These days she sells mostly firming creams for buttocks and carotene capsules because that's what brings in the most cash; she likes to say that she has 'optimised the potential of her health and beauty section'.

My sister-in-law Carine is fairly predictable.

When we heard about our stroke of luck – that we were about to have a purveyor of anti-wrinkle creams in our own family, a licensed Clinique vendor and Guerlain reseller – my sister Lola and I fell on her with shrieks of joy. Oh! What a warm welcome we gave her that day! We promised that from then on we would always go to her for our shopping, and we were even willing to call her Doctor or Professor Lariot-Molinoux so we'd be in her good books.

We'd even take the RER just to go out to see her! That's really a big deal for Lola and me, to take the train all the way out to Poissy.

Whenever we go out beyond the Boulevards des Maréchaux, we begin to feel a bit peculiar.

But there was no need to go out there because she took us by the arm at the end of that first Sunday dinner and confessed, lowering her eyes, 'You know … uh … I can't give you any discount because … uh … if I start with you, after that … well, you understand … after that I … after that you don't know where it will end, do you?' 'Not even a teeny tiny percentage?' replied Lola with a laugh. 'Not even any samples?' 'Oh, yes … yes, samples, yes. No problem.'

And when Carine left that day, clinging to our brother so he wouldn't fly away, Lola muttered as she blew kisses all the while from the balcony, 'She can stick her samples you-know-where.'

I totally agreed with her, and we shook out the tablecloth, and changed the subject.

Now we never stop teasing her about it. Every time we see her, I tell her about my friend Sandrine who is a flight attendant and the discounts she can get us at the duty-free.

For example:

'Hey, Carine, give me a price for Estée Lauder's Double Exfoliating Nitrogen Generator with Vitamin B12.'

You should see our Carine, lost in thought. She concentrates, closes her eyes, thinks of her list, calculates her margin, deducts the VAT, and eventually goes: 'Forty-five?'

I turn to Lola. 'Do you remember how much you paid?'

'Hmm … Sorry? What are you talking about?'

'Estée Lauder's Double Exfoliating Nitrogen Generator with Vitamin B12, the one Sandrine brought back for you the other day?'

'What about it?'

'How much did you pay?'

'Gosh, how do you expect me to remember? Around twenty euros, I think.'

Carine repeats what Lola has said, choking on her words. 'Twenty euros! Estée Lauder's D-E-N-G with Vitamin B12! Are you sure about that?'

'I think so.'

'I'm sorry, but at that price it's got to be fake! What a shame, girls, you've been taken for a ride. They often put Nivea in a counterfeit jar and no one's the wiser. I hate to tell you,' she insists, triumphant, 'but your cream is just some old rubbish. Absolute rubbish!'

Lola looks totally devastated. 'Are you sure?'

'Ab-so-lutely sure. I know what the production costs are, after all! They only use essential oils at Estée—'

This is where I turn to my sister and say, 'You don't happen to have it with you, do you?'

'Have what?'

'The cream.'

'No, I don't think so … Oh, yes! I just might … Wait, let me look in my bag.'

She comes back with a jar and hands it to the expert.

Said expert puts on her half-moon glasses and inspects the offending item from every angle. We watch her in silence, waiting with bated breath, vaguely uneasy.

'Well, Doctor?' ventures Lola.

'Yes, yes, it's Estée Lauder all right ... I recognise the smell ... and the texture. Lauder has a very special texture. It's incredible. How much did you say you paid? Twenty euros? That's incredible,' sighs Carine, putting her glasses back in their case, and the case back in her Biotherm pouch, and the Biotherm pouch back in her Tod's handbag. 'That's incredible! That must be cost price. How do they expect the rest of us to survive if they undercut prices like that? That's unfair practices. No more, no less. It's ... there's no more margin so they ... It's downright disgusting. It saddens me, you know ...'

Carine is utterly perplexed. She consoles herself by stirring sugarless sugar into a coffee without caffeine.

After that, the hardest part is to keep our cool as far as the kitchen, but when we finally get there, we begin cackling like turkey hens on heat. If our mother happens to walk by, she says despairingly, 'You two can be so nasty,' and Lola replies, offended, 'Hey, what do you mean? I actually paid seventy-two euros for that piece of shit!' And we

15

stand over the dishwasher splitting our sides with laughter.

'Well, that's good, with everything you won last night you'll be able to contribute to the petrol, for once.'

'Petrol AND *péage*,' I said, rubbing my nose.

I couldn't see her, but I could sense her smug little smile and both hands placed nice and flat on her tightly squeezed knees.

I raised my hips to pull a big note out of my jeans pocket.

'Put that away,' said my brother.

Up she piped: 'But, uh ... really, Simon, I don't see why—'

'I said put it away,' my brother said, without raising his voice.

She opened her mouth, closed it, wriggled a little, opened her mouth again, dusted off her thigh, fiddled with her sapphire, inspected her nails, opened her mouth to say something ... and then closed it again.

Things were not going too smoothly. If she was keeping her mouth shut, it meant they'd had a fight. If she was keeping her mouth shut, it meant that my brother had raised his voice.

Which is a rare thing.

My brother never gets annoyed, never says anything bad about anybody, hasn't an unkind bone in his body, and does not judge his fellow man. My brother is from another planet. Venus, maybe.

We adore him. We ask him: 'How do you manage to stay so calm?' He shrugs his shoulders. 'I don't know.' We ask him again: 'Don't you ever feel like letting go sometimes? Saying really mean, nasty things?'

'But that's why I have you, gorgeous,' he replies, with an angelic smile.

Yes, we adore him. In fact, everybody adores him. Our nannies, his teachers, his professors, his colleagues at work, his neighbours … everybody.

When we were younger, we'd sprawl on the carpet in his bedroom, listening to his records and smothering him with kisses while he did our homework, and we played at imagining our future. Our predictions for Simon: 'You are too nice ... some evil cow will get her claws into you.'

Bingo.

I had a pretty good idea why they'd been arguing. It was probably because of me. I could reproduce their conversation down to the last sigh.

Yesterday afternoon, I asked my brother if they could give me a lift. 'What a question,' he said, politely offended, on the phone. After that, the little love must have thrown her tantrum, because coming to pick me up meant a major detour. My brother must have shrugged his shoulders, and she'd have laid it on even thicker. 'But, darling, from her place to the road for Limousin ... Place Clichy is not exactly a short-cut, as far as I know.'

He had to force himself to be firm, they went to bed angry, and she slept at Hotel Cold Shoulder.

She got up in a bad mood. While drinking her organic chicory, she started up again. 'No, really, your lazy sister could have made the effort and come out here. Honestly, it's hardly her work that's wearing her out, is it?'

He didn't react. He was studying the map.

She went to sulk in her Kaufman & Broad bathroom (I remember our first visit. With some sort of purple chiffon scarf around her neck, she was twirling about among her pot plants and giving a running commentary on her Petit Trianon, absolutely gushing. 'Here we have the kitchen ... so functional. And now the dining room ... utterly convivial. And as for the living room ... so versatile. Here's Léo's bedroom ... isn't it playful? Now this is the laundry room ... just indispensable. And this is the bathroom ... double, obviously. And as for our bedroom ... so luminous. Here's ...' It was as if she wanted to sell it to us. Simon drove us back to the station and just as we were leaving, we said, 'You've got a beautiful house.' 'Yes, it's functional,' he echoed, nodding his head. Neither Lola nor Vincent nor I uttered a single word on the way back. We were all kind of sad, each in our own corner; we were probably thinking the same thing, that we had lost our older brother, and that life would be a lot tougher without him), and then, she must have looked at her watch at least ten times between their house and my street, she must have groaned at every traffic

light, and when finally she hooted the horn –
because I'm sure she's the one who hooted – I
didn't hear them.

Oh woe, oh woe is me.

My dear Simon, I am so sorry to have put you
through all that.

Next time, I'll make other arrangements, I
promise you.

I'll do better. I'll go to bed early. I won't drink
any more. I won't play cards.

By next time, I'll have settled down, you know.
Of course I will. I'll find someone. A nice middle
class boy. An only son. A man who's got a driving
licence and a Toyota that runs on rapeseed oil.

I'll get myself one who works at the post office,
because his dad works at the post office, who'll
put in his twenty-nine hours a week and is never
off sick. A non-smoker. That's just what I'll put
on my Match.com profile. You don't believe me?
Well, you'll see. Why are you laughing, you idiot?

That way I won't pester you any more on
Saturday mornings to go to the country. I'll tell
my little sweetie pie from the post office, 'Hey,

Sweetie Pie! Will you drive me to my cousin's wedding with your beautiful sat nav that even has Corsica and Martinique and Tahiti?' and at a stroke, problem solved, all taken care of.

And why are you laughing like a fool, now? Do you think I'm not clever enough to manage the way other people do? To find myself a nice guy with a yellow cardigan and a Disneyland Paris badge? A fiancé I can go and buy Celio boxer shorts for during my lunch break? Oh, yes, just thinking about it makes me go all wobbly … a decent sort. Serious. Simple. Batteries included, not to mention the building society passbook.

And he'd never worry about things. And his main concern would be to compare prices in-store with the ones in the catalogue and he'd say, 'You know, darling, the difference between Casto and Leroy Merlin is really just the service … '

And we'll enter the house through the basement so as not to get the hall dirty. And we'll leave our shoes at the bottom of the stairs so as not to get the stairway dirty. And we'll be friends with the neighbours, who will be incredibly nice. And we'll have a built-in barbecue and it will be really great for the kids, because the housing estate will be super safe like my sister-in-law says and …

Oh, bliss.

It was too awful. I fell asleep.

I stumbled out onto the forecourt of a petrol station somewhere on the outskirts of Orléans. Feeling groggy as hell. Woozy and drooly. I had trouble keeping my eyes open and my hair felt incredibly heavy. I even put my hand up to it, just to make sure it really was hair.

Simon was waiting by the till. Carine was powdering her nose.

I stationed myself by the coffee machine.

It took me at least thirty seconds to realise that my cup was ready. I drank it without sugar and without much conviction. I must have pressed the wrong button. Wasn't there a weird faintly tomatoey taste to my cappuccino?

Oh, boy. It was going to be a long day.

We got back in the car without saying a word. Carine took a wet wipe from her make-up bag to disinfect her hands.

Carine always disinfects her hands when she's been in a public place.

For hygiene's sake.

Because Carine actually *sees* the germs.

She can see their furry little legs and their horrible mouths.

That's why she never takes the métro. She doesn't like trains either. She can't help but think about the people who put their feet on the seats and stick their bogeys under the armrest.

Her kids are not allowed to sit on a bench or to touch the railings. She has major issues about going to the playground. And issues about letting them use the slide. She has issues with the trays at McDonald's and she has *a ton* of issues about swapping Pokémon cards. She completely freaks out with butchers who don't wear gloves or little salesgirls who don't use tongs to serve her her croissant. She hates it when the school organises group picnics or outings to the swimming pool and all the kids have to hold hands as a sure way of passing on their fungal infections.

Life, for Carine, is exhausting.

The business with the disinfectant wipes really gets up my nose.

The way she always thinks other people must be swarming with germs. The way she always peers at their fingernails when she shakes hands. The way she never trusts anyone. Always hiding behind her scarf. Always telling her kids to be careful.

Don't touch. It's dirty.

Get your hands out of there.

Don't share.

Don't go out in the street.

Don't sit on the ground or I'll smack you!

Always washing their hands. Always washing their mouths. Always making sure they pee exactly ten centimetres above the bowl, dead centre, and that they never ever let their lips touch someone's cheek when they go to kiss them. Always judging the other mothers by the colour of their kids' ears.

Always.

Always judging.

There's something rather unpleasant about it all. What's worse, when you go to lunch at her family's, they soon feel free mid-meal to start badmouthing Arabs.

Carine's dad calls them towelheads.

He says, 'I pay taxes so those towelheads can have ten kids.'

He says, 'What I'd do with 'em, I'd stick 'em all in a boat and torpedo the whole lot of them, every last parasite, I would.'

And he likes to say, 'France is full of work-shy benefit cheats. The country's going to the dogs.'

And often, to finish, it goes like this: 'I work the first six months of the year for my family and the next six for the state, so don't go talking to me about poor people and the unemployed, okay? I work one day out of two so Mamadou can knock up his ten wives, so don't go lecturing me, okay?'

There was one lunch in particular. I don't like remembering it. It was for little Alice's baptism. We were all at Carine's parents' place near Le Mans.

Her father runs a Casino (the supermarket, not the Las Vegas variety) and that day, when I saw him down at the end of his little paved driveway between his artsy-fartsy wrought-iron lamp and his gleaming Audi, I really understood the meaning of the word complacent. That mixture of stupidity and arrogance. His unshakeable self-satisfaction. That blue cashmere sweater stretched over his huge gut and that weird – really warm – way he has of holding his hand out to you even though he already hates you.

I'm ashamed when I think back to that lunch. I'm ashamed and I'm not the only one. Lola and Vincent aren't proud of themselves either, I don't think.

Simon wasn't there when the conversation began to degenerate. He was out in the garden building a cabin for his son.

He must be used to it. He must know that it's better just to get out of there when fat Jacquot starts sounding off.

Simon is like us: he doesn't like shouting matches at the end of a nice meal; he hates conflict and runs like hell from power struggles. He says it's a waste of good energy and that you have to keep your strength for more worthwhile struggles in life. That with people like his father-in-law, you're fighting a losing battle.

And when you talk to him about the rise of the extreme right, he shakes his head. 'Oh, you know … they're just the dregs on the bottom of the lake. What can you do, it's only human. Best leave well enough alone, otherwise they'll rise to the surface.'

How can he stand those family lunches? How can he even help his father-in-law trim his hedge?

He concentrates on Léo's cabins.

He concentrates on the moment he'll take his little boy by the hand and they'll go off together into the deep and silent woods.

I'm ashamed because on that particular day we didn't dare say a thing.

Once again we didn't dare say a thing. We didn't react to the words of that rabid shopkeeper who'll never see beyond his own distant navel.

We didn't contradict him, or leave the table. We went on slowly chewing every mouthful, thinking it was enough just to register what a jerk the guy was whilst doing our very best to wrap ourselves in what might remain of our dignity.

How pathetic we were. Cowards, incredible cowards.

Why are we like that, all four of us? Why are we so intimidated by people who shout louder than others? Why do aggressive people make us go completely to pieces?

What is wrong with us? Where does a good upbringing end and spinelessness begin?

We've talked about it a lot. We beat our breasts over the pizza crusts and makeshift ashtrays. We don't need anyone to force us to. We're big enough to go about it ourselves, and no matter how many empty bottles we have at the end, we always come to the same conclusion. That if we are like this – silent and determined but absolutely useless when it comes to bigots like him – it is precisely because we haven't got a shred of self-confidence. We don't love ourselves.

We don't believe in ourselves, that is.

We don't think we're all that important.

Not even important enough to argue the toss with old man Molinoux. Or to believe for one second that our protesting could ever have any influence on his line of thought. Or to hope that a gesture of disgust like tossing our napkins onto the table or knocking over our chairs might have the slightest impact on the ways of the world.

What would that good taxpayer have thought if we had given him a piece of our mind and left his house with our heads held high? He would simply have battered his wife all evening with remarks like: 'What complete pricks. Total pricks. I mean, have you ever seen such a hopeless bunch of pricks?'

And why should the poor woman be subjected to that?

There were twenty people enjoying themselves – who were we to spoil the party?

So you might say that it isn't cowardice. You might allow that it's actually wisdom. Acknowledge that we know when to stand back. That we don't like to make things worse. That we're more honest than all those people who protest all the time but never manage to change a thing.

Or at least that's what we tell each other, to make ourselves feel better. We remind each other that we're young and already we have no illusions.

And that we're head and shoulders above the ant-hill so stupidity can't really reach us up here. We don't really give a damn. We have other things, each other for a start. We are rich in other ways.

All we have to do is look inside.

We have a lot going on in our heads. Stuff that's light years from that man's racist ranting. There's music, and literature. There are walks to go on, hands to hold, secret dens. Bits of shooting stars scribbled onto credit card receipts, pages torn out of books, happy memories and horrible ones. Songs with refrains that are just on the tip of our tongues. Messages we've kept, blockbusters we loved reading, marshmallow teddy bears and scratched vinyl records. Our childhood, our lonely times, our first feelings and plans for the future. All that staying up late, and all those doors held open for us. Buster Keaton's antics. Armand Robin's brave letter to the Gestapo and Michel Leiris's battering ram of clouds. The scene where Clint Eastwood turns round and says, *'One thing though … don't kid yourself, Francesca …'* and the one in *The Best of Youth* where Nicola Carati stands up for his patients at the trial of their tor-

turer. The dances on Bastille Day in Villiers. The
scent of quinces in the cellar. Our grandparents,
Monsieur Racine's sabre and gleaming breast-
plate, our provincial fantasies and nights before
our exams. Our favourite comics: Mam'zelle
Jeanne's raincoat when she climbs on behind
Gaston on his motorbike, or François Bourgeon's
Les Passagers du vent. The opening lines of the
book by André Gorz dedicated to his wife, which
Lola read to me last night on the telephone when
we'd just spent ages saying we were finished with
love, yet again: 'You're about to turn eighty-two.
You're two inches shorter, you weigh only seven
stone, and you are still beautiful, gracious and
desirable.' Marcello Mastroianni in *Dark Eyes*;
gowns by Cristóbal Balenciaga. The way the
horses would smell of dust and dry bread when
you got off the school bus in the evening. The La-
lannes, each working in their own studio with a
garden in between. The night we spray painted
Rue des Vertus, and the time we slipped a stinking
herring skin under the terrace of the restaurant
where that stupid ass Mr Teflon worked. And the
time we rode on the back of a truck, face down
on sheets of cardboard, and Vincent read us all of

Robert Linhart's *L'Établi* out loud. Simon's face when he heard Björk for the first time in his life, or Monteverdi, in the car park of the Macumba.

So much silliness, and regret, and the soap bubbles at Lola's godfather's funeral …

Our lost loves, our torn-up letters, and our friends on the end of the telephone. All those unforgettable nights, and how we were forever rearranging our stuff, and all the strangers we knocked into all those times we had to run to catch a bus that wasn't going to wait for us anyway.

All of that, and more.

Enough to keep our souls alive.

Enough to know not to try to talk back to morons.

Let them die.

They will anyway.

They'll die all alone while we're at the cinema.

That's what we tell ourselves so we'll feel better about not having got up and left the table that day.

Then there's the obvious fact that all of it — our apparent indifference, our discretion and our weakness, too — is our parents' fault.

It's their fault — or should I say it's thanks to them.

Because they're the ones who taught us about books and music. Who talked to us about other things and forced us to see things in a different light. To aim higher and further. But they also forgot to give us confidence, because they thought that it would just come naturally. That we had a special gift for life, and compliments might spoil our egos.

They got it wrong.

The confidence never came.

So here we are. Sublime losers. We just sit there in silence while the loudmouths get their way, and any brilliant response we might have come up with is nipped in the bud, and all we're left with is a vague desire to be sick.

Maybe it was all the whipped cream we ate.

I remember how one day we were all together, the whole family, on a beach near Hossegor — because we rarely went anywhere together as a family – family with a capital F, that wasn't really our style – our pop (our father never wanted us to call him Papa and so when people were surprised we would say it was because of May 1968. That was a pretty good excuse, we thought, 'May '68', like a secret code; it was as if we were saying, 'It's because he's from planet Zorg') – so our pop, as I was saying, must have looked up and said, 'Now children, you see this beach?'

(Any idea how huge the Côte d'Argent is?)

'Well, do you know what you are, you children, on the scale of the universe?'

(Yeah! Kids who aren't allowed any doughnuts!)

'You are this grain of sand. Just this one, right here. And nothing more.'

We believed him.
Our loss.

'What's that smell?' said Carine.

I was spreading Madame Rashid's paste all over my legs.

'What … what on earth is that stuff?'

'I'm not sure exactly. I think it's honey or caramel mixed with wax and spices.'

'Oh my God, that's horrible! That is disgusting! And you're going to do that here?'

'Where else can I do it? I can't go to the wedding like this. I look like a yeti.'

My sister-in-law turned away with a sigh.

'Be very careful of the seat. Simon, turn off the air conditioning so I can open the window.'

Please, I muttered, my teeth clenched.

Madame Rashid had wrapped this huge lump of what looked like Turkish delight in a damp cloth. 'Next time come see me, I take care of you. I do your little love garden. After you see how he like it, your man, when I make it all gone, he go crazy with you and he give you anything you want,' she assured me with a wink.

I smiled. Just a faint smile. I'd just made a mark on the armrest and was juggling Kleenex. What a mess.

'And are you going to get dressed in the car, too?'

'We'll stop somewhere just before. Hey, Simon? Can you find me a little side road somewhere?'

'One that smells of hazelnuts?'

'I should hope so!'

'And Lola?' asked Carine.

'What about Lola?'

'Is she coming?'

'I don't know.'

'You don't know?' She looked startled.

'No. I don't know.'

'This is unbelievable. Nobody ever knows anything with you guys. It's always the same thing. A complete bohemian shambles. Can't you get your act together for once? Just a little bit?'

'I spoke to her on the phone yesterday,' I said curtly. 'She wasn't feeling too good and still didn't know whether she could make it.'

'Well, well, what a surprise.'

Oooh, how I disliked that condescending tone of hers.

'What's surprising about it?' I said, through clenched teeth.

'Oh dear! Nothing. Nothing surprises me any more with you lot. And if Lola is feeling that way, it's her fault, too. It's what she wanted, isn't it? She really has a knack for ending up in the most incredible fixes. You don't just go around—'

I could see Simon frowning in the rear-view mirror.

'Well, as far as I'm concerned ...'

Yes. Exactly. As far as you're concerned ...

'... the problem with Lo—'

'Stop!' I exploded, cutting across her. 'Stop right there. I didn't get enough sleep, so ... leave it for later.'

Then she got all huffy. 'Oh, well! No one can ever say a thing in this family. The least little comment about any of you and the other three rush to put a knife to your throat; it's ridiculous.'

Simon was trying to catch my eye.

'And you think that's funny, do you? Both of you, you think it's funny, don't you? It's unbelievable. Completely childish. I'm entitled to my opinion, aren't I? Since you won't listen and no one can say a thing to you, and no one ever does say a thing, you're untouchable. You never stop to question yourselves. Well, I'm going to give you a piece of my mind—'

But we don't want a piece of your mind, sweetheart.

'I think this protectionism of yours, this way you have of acting all "to hell with the rest of you" won't do you any favours. It's not the least bit constructive.'

'But *what is* constructive here on earth, Carine love?'

'Oh please, spare me! Not that, too. Don't start on your pseudo-Socrates disillusioned philosophers act. It's pathetic, at your age. And have you finished with that gunk, it really is revolting—'

'Yeah, yeah,' I assured her, rolling the ball over my white calves, 'I'm almost done.'

'Aren't you going to use some sort of cream afterwards? Your pores are in a state of shock now; you've got to remoisturise your skin otherwise you'll be covered in little red spots until tomorrow.'

'Damn, I forgot to bring anything.'

'Don't you have your face cream?'

'No.'

'Or moisturiser?'

'No.'

'Night cream?'

'No.'

'You didn't bring anything?'

She was horrified.

'I did. I brought a toothbrush, and some tooth-paste, and L'Heure Bleue, and some condoms, and mascara, and a tube of lip-balm.'

She was shattered.

'That is all you have in your toilet bag?'

'Uh … it's in my handbag. I don't have a toilet bag.'

She sighed, and started rummaging in her make-up bag, and she handed me a big white tube.

'Here, put some of this on.'

I thanked her with a genuine smile. She was pleased. She may be a first-class pain but she does like to please others. Credit where credit is due.

And she really doesn't like to leave pores in a state of shock. It breaks her heart.

After a few minutes she added, 'Garance?'

'Mm-hmm?'

'You know what I think is deeply unfair?'

'The profit that Seph—'

'No, that you'll be lovely no matter what. Just a little bit of lip gloss and a touch of mascara, and you'll be beautiful. It hurts me to say it, but it's true.'

I was floored. It was the first time in years she'd said anything nice to me. I could have kissed her, but then right away she ruined it.

'Hey, don't use up the whole tube! It's not L'Oréal, I'll have you know.'

That's Carine all over. No sooner does she suspect you might catch her red-handed in a moment of weakness than, systematically, after doing you a favour, she has to make a cutting remark.

Pity. She's missing out on a lot of good moments. It would have been a good moment for her if I'd flung my arms round her neck without warning. A great big smacker, between two trucks ... But no. She always has to spoil everything.

I often think I ought to invite her to live with me for a day or two to give her a few lessons in life.

So that she could let her guard down for once, let herself go, roll up her sleeves and forget about other people's imperfections.

It makes me sad to see her like that, straitjacketed by all her prejudices and incapable of tenderness. And then I remember that she was raised by the dashing Jacques and Francine Molinoux at the bottom of a dead-end street in the residential outskirts of Le Mans and I figure that, all things considered, she isn't doing so badly after all.

The cease-fire didn't last, and Simon was used for target practice.

'You're driving too fast. Lock the doors, we're getting near the *péage*. What on earth is that on the radio? I didn't mean twenty miles an hour though, did I? Why'd you turn the air con off? Watch out for those bikers. Are you sure you've got the right map? Can't you read the road signs, please? It's so stupid, I'm sure petrol cost less back there … Be careful round the bends – can't you see I'm painting my nails? Hey … are you doing it on purpose, or what?'

I can just make out the back of my brother's neck in the hollow space of his headrest. That fine, straight neck, and close-cropped hair.

I wonder how he can stand it, I wonder if he ever dreams of tying her to a tree and running off as fast as his legs can carry him.

Why does she speak to him like that? Does she even know who she's talking to? Does she know that the man sitting next to her was the god of scale models? The ace of Meccano sets? A Lego System genius?

A patient little boy who could spend several months building the most incredible planet, with dried lichen for the ground, and hideous creatures made from bread rolled in spiders' webs?

A stubborn little tyke who entered every contest and won nearly all of them: Nesquik, Ovaltine, Babybel, Caran d'Ache, Kellogg's and the Mickey Mouse Club?

One year, his sand castle was so beautiful that the judges disqualified him: they claimed he'd had help. He cried all afternoon and our granddad had to take him to the crêperie to console him. He drank three whole mugs of cider one after the other.

First time he ever got roaring drunk.

Does she even know that for months her good little lapdog of a hubby wore a satin Superman cape day and night that he folded up conscientiously in his schoolbag whenever it was time to go through the gate into the playground? He was the only boy who knew how to repair the photocopy machine in the town hall. And he was the only one who'd ever seen Mylène Carois's knickers – she was the butcher's daughter, Carois &

Fils. (He hadn't dared tell her that he was not all that interested.)

Simon Lariot, a discreet man, who'd always made his own sweet way, gracefully, without bothering a soul.

Who never threw tantrums, or whined, or asked for a thing. Who went through his university prep classes and got onto a top engineering course without ever grinding his teeth or resorting to tranquillisers. Who didn't want to make a big deal when he did well, and turned bright red when the headmistress of the Lycée Stendhal kissed him in the street to congratulate him.

The same big boy who can laugh like an idiot for exactly twenty minutes when he's smoking a joint and who knows *every single* journey of *every single* spaceship in *Star Wars*.

I'm not saying he's a saint, I'm saying he's better than one.

Why, then? Why does he let people walk all over him? It's a mystery to me. I've lost track of the number of times I've wanted to shake him, to open his eyes and get him to pound his fist on the table. Countless times.

One day Lola tried. He sent her packing and barked that it was his life, after all.

Which is true. It's his life. But we're the ones who are saddened by it.

Which is idiotic, in a way. We've got more than enough to keep us busy on our own turf.

He opens up the most with Vincent. Because of the Internet. They're in touch the whole time, sending each other corny jokes and links for websites where they can find old vinyl LPs and second-hand guitars and other model enthusiasts. Simon has made great friends with a guy in Massachusetts; they swap photos of their respective remote-control boats. His name is Cecil (Simon can't pronounce it right; he says See-sull) W. Thurlington and he lives in a big house on Martha's Vineyard.

Lola and I think it sounds really chic. Martha's Vineyard … 'The cradle of the Kennedys', as they say in *Paris-Match*.

We have this fantasy where we take the plane and then go up to Cecil's private beach and we shout, 'Yoo-hoo! Darling See-sull! We are Simon's sisters! We are so very *en-chant-té*!'

We picture him wearing a navy-blue blazer, with a dusty-pink cotton sweater thrown over his shoulders, and off-white linen slacks. Straight out of a Ralph Lauren ad.

When we threaten Simon with our disgraceful plan, he tends to lose some of his cool.

'Hey, are you doing it on purpose or what?'

'Well, how many coats do you have to put on, anyway?' he says eventually.

'Three.'

'Three coats?'

'Base, colour and fixer.'

'Oh.'

'Be careful, and at least warn me when you're about to brake.'

He raises his eyebrows. No. Correction. One eyebrow.

What can he be thinking when he raises his right eyebrow like that?

We ate rubbery sandwiches at one of those motor-way service stations. It was revolting. I'd wanted us to have a *plat du jour* at a roadside café but 'they don't know how to wash the lettuce'. True. I'd forgotten. So, three vacuum-packed sandwiches, please. (Infinitely more hygienic.)

'It may not be good, but at least we know what we're eating!'

That's one way of looking at it.

We were sitting outside next to the dustcarts. You could hear *brrrrammm* and *brrrroommm* every two seconds but I wanted to smoke a cigarette and Carine cannot stand the smell of tobacco.

'I have to go to the toilet,' she announced, with a pained expression. 'I don't suppose it's too luxurious.'

'Why don't you go in the grass?' I asked.

'In front of everyone? Are you crazy?'

'Just go a little bit further that way. I'll come with you if you want.'

'No.'

'Why not?'

'I'll get my shoes dirty.'

'I don't think so, what's a few drops.'

She got up without deigning to answer.

'You know, Carine,' I said solemnly, 'the day you learn to enjoy having a wee in the grass, you'll be a much happier person.'

She took her wet wipes.

'I'm fine as I am, thank you.'

I turned to my brother. He was staring at the cornfield as if he were trying to count every single ear. He didn't look too good.

'You okay?'

'I'm okay,' he replied, without turning round.

'Doesn't look it.'

He was rubbing his face.

'I'm tired.'

'What of?'

'Of everything.'

'You? I don't believe you.'

'And yet it's true.'

'Is it your work?'

'My work. My life. Everything.'

'Why are you telling me this?'

'Why wouldn't I tell you?'

He had his back to me again.

'Hey, Simon! What's going on? Don't talk like this. You're the hero of the family, in case you need reminding.'

'Well, yeah, that's kind of the problem. The hero is tired.'

I was speechless. This was the first time I'd ever seen him in such a state.

If Simon was beginning to have doubts, where were we headed?

Just then – and to me this was a miracle, although on the other hand it doesn't surprise me and I kiss the patron saint of brothers and sisters who has been watching over us now for nearly thirty-five years, and who has never been out of work, poor guy – his mobile rang.

It was Lola, who had finally made up her mind, and was asking him if he could stop and pick her up at the station in Châteauroux.

Our spirits immediately revived. Simon put his phone back in his pocket and asked me for a cigarette. Carine came back, scrubbing her arms right up to her elbows. She immediately reminded her husband of the precise number of cancer victims who had died because of … He gave a limp wave of his hand as if he were brushing away a fly and she walked off, coughing.

Lola was coming. Lola would be with us. Lola hadn't let us down, and the rest of the world could just go hang.

Simon put on his sunglasses.

He was smiling.

His little Lola was on the train.

They have this special thing between them. First of all, they're closest in age, only eighteen months apart, and then they really were *children* together.

They were the ones who were always getting up to mischief. Lola had an irrepressible imagination and Simon was pliant (already). They ran away. They got lost. They got into fights, tormented each other, made up. Maman likes to tell us how Lola would needle him all the time, always going into his bedroom to bug him, grabbing the book from his hands or kicking something straight into his Playmobil. My sister doesn't like to recall these acts of war (she worries she's being tarred with the same brush as Carine), so then our mother senses that she'd better change tack and she adds that Lola was always eager for something new; she'd invite all the kids in the neighbourhood and invent all kinds of fun games. She was like a really cool Scout pack leader who could come up with a thousand ideas a minute, and she watched over her big brother like a broody hen. She'd make all sorts of inedible snacks for him with mustard and Nutella and she'd come and prise him from his Lego when it was time for *UFO Robot Grendizer* or *Captain Harlock* on the television.

Lola and Simon grew up during the Golden Age. When we lived in Villiers, out in the sticks, and our parents were happy together. For them the world began outside the front door and ended on the other side of the village.

They would streak across fields pursued by imaginary bulls, and creep into abandoned houses haunted by ghosts that weren't imaginary at all.

They would ring old Madame Margeval's bell, until it drove her crazy; they destroyed the hunters' traps; they pissed into washtubs, nicked the teacher's dirty magazines, stole bangers, set off mammoth ones, and rescued little kittens that some bastard had sealed up alive in a plastic bag.

Bam. Seven kittens all at once. You can imagine how happy our father was!

And the day the Tour de France came through our village Lola and Simon went and bought fifty baguettes and sold sandwiches by the dozen. With their earnings they bought practical jokes and tricks, and sixty packets of Malabar bubble gum, and a skipping rope for me, and a little trumpet for Vincent (already!) and the latest comic book.

Yes, they had a different childhood. They knew what a rowlock was, and they smoked creepers and knew the taste of gooseberries. And the event that made the greatest impact on them, was recorded, in secret, on the back of the shed door.

Today Ar April 8 we saw the preist wearing shorts.

Then they went through our parents' divorce together. Vincent and I were still too little. We only really worked out what a raw deal we were getting on the day it came to move house. But they'd been able to witness the entire show. They would get up in the middle of the night and go and sit side by side at the top of the stairs to listen to the 'discussion'. One night Pop knocked over the huge kitchen cupboard and Maman drove off in the car.

While ten steps up they sat sucking their thumbs.

It's stupid to go on telling that side of the story; they were close for any number of reasons that, in the long run, meant more than the tough times. But still …

For Vincent and me it was completely different. We were city brats. Less cycling and more time in front of the box. We had no idea how to stick on a rubber repair patch but we did know how to dodge ticket inspectors or repair a skateboard or sneak into the cinema through the emergency exit.

And then Lola got sent to boarding school, and there was no one around any more to fill our heads with whispered mischief or chase after us in the garden.

We wrote to each other every week. She was my beloved older sister. I idealised her; I sent her drawings and wrote poems to her. When she came home she would ask me whether Vincent had behaved himself during her absence. Of course not, I'd say, of course not. And I'd describe in detail all the horrible things I'd had to undergo the previous week. At which point, to my supreme satisfaction, she'd drag him into the bathroom to acquaint him with the riding crop.

The louder my brother screamed, the wider I grinned.

And then one day, to make it even better, I wanted to see him suffer. To my complete, flabbergasted horror, I burst in to find my sister whipping a bolster, while Vincent bleated in time, reading his Boule et Bill comic book. A major disappointment. On that day, Lola fell from her pedestal.

Which turned out to be a good thing. Now we were the same height.

Nowadays she's my best friend. We're sort of like Montaigne and La Boétie, for example. Because she is who she is, and I am who I am. The fact that this young woman of thirty-two years of age is also my older sister is totally beside the point. Well, maybe not totally; it's just fortunate we didn't have to waste time trying to find each other.

She's really into Montaigne's *Essays* – she likes grand theories, the notion that one is punished for stubbornly held opinions, and philosophy is just learning how to die. Give me La Boétie's *Discourse of Voluntary Servitude* any time – infinite abuse and all those tyrants who are only great because we kneel before them. She'll take true knowledge, I'll take tribunals. We are both so grown and accustomed to be always the other's double in all places and in all things, that without the other methinks I am no more than half of myself.

And yet we are very different. She is afraid of her own shadow; I sit on mine. She copies out sonnets, I download samples. She admires painters, I prefer photographers. She never tells you what is in her heart, I speak my mind. She avoids conflict, I like things to be perfectly clear. She likes to be 'a little bit tipsy', I prefer to drink. She doesn't like going out, I don't like going home. She doesn't know how to have fun, I don't know when it's time to get some sleep. She hates gambling, I hate losing. Her embrace is all-encompassing, my kindness has its limits. She never gets annoyed, I'm forever blowing a gasket.

She says the world belongs to early risers, I beg her to keep her voice down. She's romantic, I'm pragmatic. She got married, I flitter and flirt. She can't sleep with a guy unless she's in love, I can't sleep with a guy unless there's a condom. She needs me and I need her.

She doesn't judge, she takes me as I am. With my grey complexion and my black thoughts. Or my rosebud complexion and my rose-tinted thoughts. Lola knows how it feels to lust after a pea coat or a pair of heels. She completely understands how much fun it can be to go over your credit card limit then feel guilty as hell when the bill comes. Lola spoils me. She holds the curtain for me when I'm in the fitting room, and she always tells me I'm beautiful and no, not at all, it doesn't make my bum look huge. She asks, every time, how my love life is going, and pulls a face when I tell her about my lovers.

Whenever we haven't seen each other for a long time she takes me to a brasserie, Bofinger or Balzar, to look at the guys. I focus on the ones at nearby tables; she zeroes in on the waiters. She is fascinated by those gangling lads in tight waistcoats. She can't take her eyes off them, she imagines life stories for them straight out of a Claude Sautet film, and she dissects their perfectly trained mannerisms. The funny thing is that at some point you always see one of them leaving at the end of his shift. And then she wonders what she ever saw in him. Jeans or even trackie bottoms in place of the long white apron, and an offhand shout to a workmate as he takes his leave: 'Bye, Bernard!'

'Bye, Mimi. You here tomorrow?'

'Yes, worst luck. See you then.'

Lola looks down and traces patterns in the sauce on her plate with her fingertips. Another one gone, Paul, François and all the others.

We sort of lost touch for a while. She was busy with boarding school, her studies, then her wedding list, vacations at her in-laws', dinner parties.

We still knew how to hug, but we weren't at ease with each other any more. She had changed sides. Teams, rather. She wasn't playing *against* us so much as playing a game that was, well, kind of boring. A sort of stupid cricket with lots of incomprehensible rules, where you go running after something you never see but which can really hurt you … some sort of leathery thing with a cork centre. (Hey, Lola! I didn't mean to, but I've just summed it all up!)

Whereas we younger kids were still busy with a lot more basic things. A lovely lawn – hubba hubba! Drinking beer and messing around. Tall boys wearing white polo shirts – honk, honk! Kicking each other in the bum. Well, you see what I'm driving at. Not really mature enough yet for strolls around the Bassin de Neptune at Versailles.

There you have it. We'd wave to each other from a distance. She made me the godmother of her first child and I made her the trustee of my first broken heart (and how I wept, bucketfuls), but between two of these sort of major events there was not much going on. Birthdays, family lunches, a few cigarettes shared on the sly so her husband wouldn't see, a knowing look, or her head on my shoulder when we'd browse through old photos.

That was life. Her life, at any rate.

Respect.

And then she came back to us. Covered in ash, with the lunatic gaze of the pyromaniac who's just handed in his box of matches. Plaintiff in a divorce that no one expected. It has to be said she played her cards close to her chest, the minx. Everyone thought she was happy. I think we even admired her for it, for finding a way out so easily and quickly. 'Lola's got it all sorted,' we'd say, without bitterness or envy. Lola is still champ when it comes to inventing treasure hunts.

And then crash bang wallop. A change of plan.

She just showed up at my place one day, and at a time that wasn't like her at all. At bath and bedtime-story time. She was in tears, apologising. She truly believed that it was the people around her who justified her existence on this earth, and everything else – her secret life and all the little nooks and crannies of her soul – was not really that important. What was important was being cheerful and carrying your yoke as if it were the easiest thing in the world. And when things got harder, there was always solitude, drawing, and going for ever longer walks with the buggy, and the kids' books and family life that offered such a deep and comfortable refuge.

So it seemed. That little red hen in the Père Castor series was right, the perfect model of housewifely escapism.

Red Hen's the perfect housewife:
Not a speck of dust on the furniture,
The flowers all in their vases,
And carefully ironed curtains at every window.
What a treat to see her house!

Except that, here's the thing, Lola had gone out and cut that little red hen's throat.

I was stunned, like everyone else. I didn't know what to say. She'd never complained, never let on that she had her doubts, and she'd just given birth to another adorable little boy. She was loved. She had it all, as they say. 'They' being a load of idiots.

How are you supposed to react when you find out your whole solar system is out of kilter? What are you supposed to say? For Christ's sake – she was the one who'd always shown us the way. We trusted her. Or at least I trusted her. We sat on the floor for what seemed like ages, knocking back the vodka. She was in tears, and over and over she said she didn't know where the hell she was going, then she'd fall silent and burst into tears again. No matter what she decided, she'd be miserable. She could stay, or she could go: life was no longer worth living.

But the vodka was helping. Together, we managed to shake her out of her apathy. Hey! She wasn't the only one who'd been shipwrecked. When the instruction booklet is as fat as a telephone directory and you're running in circles on a lawn the size of a pocket handkerchief with no one at your side, or at least not your lawful wedded, well, when you can't take it any more, time to get out, girl!

She wasn't listening.

'And what about the kids … couldn't you hang on a bit longer, for their sake?' I eventually murmured, handing her another packet of tissues. My question dried her tears on the spot. I really didn't get it, did I? It was for their sake, this whole mess. To spare them the suffering. So that they'd never hear their parents fighting and crying in the middle of the night. Besides, you can't grow up in a house where people don't love each other any more – or can you?

No. You can't. You can grow, maybe, but not grow up.

What came after that was more sordid. Lawyers, tears, blackmail, sorrow, sleepless nights, fatigue, self-sacrifice, guilt, it hurts me more than it hurts you, aggression, recrimination, court, taking sides, appeal, discouragement, foreheads despairingly against the wall. And in the midst of it all, two little boys with clear bright eyes for whose sake she went on playing the clown, telling them her bedtime stories about farting princes and airhead princesses. This is all fairly recent, and the embers are still warm. It wouldn't take much for the sorrow she felt at the sorrow she caused to overwhelm her again, and I know there are mornings she has trouble getting out of bed. She confessed the other day that when the kids went off with their dad she stood for ages watching herself crying in the mirror in the hall.

As if she were trying to dilute herself.

That was why she didn't want to come to this wedding.

To have to deal with family. All the uncles and ageing aunts and distant cousins. All these people who haven't got divorced. Who've settled. Who've found other ways. Who'll look at her with their vaguely sympathetic expressions – or maybe they're just dismayed. Then all the theatrics: the virginal white dress, the Bach cantatas, the vows of eternal fidelity learned by heart, and the schoolboy speeches, the two hands joined on the knife of the wedding cake, and 'The Blue Danube' just as your feet are really beginning to ache. But more than anything else: the kids. Other people's kids.

The ones who'll be running all over the place all day long, their cheeks flushed from finishing the dregs in people's glasses, and stains on their best clothes, begging not to have to go to bed yet.

Kids are the whole point of family reunions – and they're our consolation for having to attend them.

They're always the nicest things to look at. They're always the first ones on the dance floor, and the only ones who will dare tell you that the cake is disgusting. They fall madly in love for the first time in their lives and fall asleep exhausted on their mothers' laps. Pierre was supposed to be a pageboy, and he'd worked out that his cybersabre would fit perfectly in his cummerbund. But Lola had got the dates on the judge's calendar wrong: it wasn't her weekend for the kids. So no little baskets, no rice battles outside the church. We had suggested she call Thierry to see if she couldn't swap weekends with him. She didn't even reply.

But now she was coming! And Vincent would be waiting for us! We'd be able to sit down at a table off to one side behind a tent, just the four of us and a few bottles we'd grab on the way, and give a running commentary on Aunt Solange's hat, or the bride's hips, or how ridiculous our cousin Hubert looked with his hired top hat jammed down over his big sticking-out ears. (His mother would never entertain the possibility of having his ears pinned back, because 'one must not undo the work of God'.) (I know. As if he were a beautiful antique.)

The clan was reuniting. It would be the four of us together again.

Trumpets, sound! Larks, sing! It was time for some sibling swashbuckling – all for one and one for … and all that jazz.

'Why are you taking this exit?'

'We're going to pick up Lola,' said Simon.

'Where?' said his wife, in a strangled voice.

'At the station in Châteauroux.'

'Is this a joke?'

'No, it's not. She'll be there in forty minutes.'

'Why didn't you tell me?'

'I forgot. She called me a little while ago.'

'When?'

'When we were at the service station.'

'I didn't hear the phone.'

'You were in the loo.'

'I see.'

'What do you see?'

'Nothing.'

Her lips said just the opposite.

'Is there a problem?' asked my brother.

'No. No problem. None at all. It's just that next time why don't you put a taxi sign on the roof of the car and be done with it?'

He didn't react. His knuckles went white.

Carine had left Léo and Alice with her mother so that, quote, *We can have a romantic weekend* dot, dot dot, close quote.

And things were definitely about to get torrid!

'And what about you ... do you intend to sleep in the same hotel room as us, too?'

'No, no,' I said, shaking my head, 'don't worry.'

'Have you booked yourself a room?'

'Well ... no.'

'Of course not. Just as I suspected.'

'But it's not a problem! We can sleep anywhere! We can go to Aunt Paule's!'

'Aunt Paule is full up. She told me on the phone the day before yesterday.'

'Well, we just won't sleep then!'

She muttered *godyerrude*, fiddling with the fringe on her pashmina.

I didn't understand.

We were out of luck. The train was ten minutes late and when finally all the passengers had disembarked there was no sign of Lola.

Simon and I prepared for the worst.

'Are you sure you didn't confuse Châteauroux and Châteaudun?' squawked the shrew.

But then – yes, look. There she was. Right at the end of the platform. She was in the last carriage; she must have boarded the train at the last minute, but there she was, walking towards us, waving her arms.

True to form and just the way I'd hoped to find her. A smile on her face, strolling along in ballet pumps, a white shirt and a pair of old jeans.

And an amazing hat. With a huge brim and a wide black grosgrain ribbon.

She hugged me. 'You look lovely,' she said. 'Have you had your hair cut?' She hugged Simon and stroked his back then she took off her hat so she wouldn't mess up Carine's hair.

She'd had to travel in the guard's van as there was nowhere to put her sombrero so she asked us

if we wouldn't mind stopping at the station buf-
fet for her to buy a sandwich. Carine looked at
her watch and I took advantage of that to grab a
trashy magazine.

The celebrity press. Our guilty pleasure.

We got into the car, and Lola asked her sister-
in-law if she would be willing to have her hat on
her lap. Oh, no problem, said she, with a some-
what forced smile. No problem.

My sister raised her chin as if to ask, What's going on? And I raised my eyes to heaven to reply,
same old.

She smiled and asked Simon to put on some
music.

Carine replied that she had a headache.

I smiled, too.

Then Lola asked whether anyone had any nail
polish for her toenails. She asked again: no answer. Finally our favourite pharmacist handed
her a little red bottle. 'Make sure you don't get
any on the seats, okay?'

Then we swapped sister stories. I'll skip that
scene. Too many in-jokes, short cuts and uproari-

ous laughter. Besides, without the soundtrack, it's meaningless.

All you sisters out there will know what I mean.

We'd arrived in the middle of nowhere, Carine was reading the map and Simon was being hauled over the coals. At some point he said, 'Give that fucking map to Garance, she's the only one who has any sense of direction in this bloody family!'

In the back, we looked at each other and frowned. Two swearwords in the same sentence, with an exclamation mark at the end. That wasn't a good sign.

Shortly before we arrived at Aunt Paule's small château, Simon came upon a little lane with black-berry bushes on either side. It reminded us of the arbours in Villiers; we rushed over to the bushes and our voices were trembling. Carine didn't bother to get out of the car and called out to re-mind us that foxes piss on blackberry bushes.

We didn't take any notice.

Our mistake ...

'Naturally. You've never heard of echinococcosis. The larvae of parasites are transmitted by urine, and—'

Mea culpa, mea maxima culpa, I lost it there for a minute. 'That's total bullshit, with bells on! Foxes can piss wherever they like, they have the entire great outdoors! Every path and hedge and tree, wherever you look, why on earth would they come and piss right here? Right on our blackberries? What the hell are you saying? That's what I can't stand. *That's* what makes me sick, people like you who always have to go spoiling everything.'

Sorry. *Mea culpa.* My fault. All my fault. And I had promised myself I would behave. I had promised myself I'd stay calm and infinitely zen. This very morning, when I was looking at myself in the mirror, I wagged my finger at my reflection. Garance, don't have a go at Carine, okay? No drama queen routine for once. But there, I blew it. I'm sorry. Sackcloth and ashes, etc. She spoiled our blackberries and the little bit of childhood we had remaining along with it. She presses all my buttons, I can't stand her. One more remark and I'd make her eat Lola's sombrero.

She must have felt the force of my fury because she closed the car door and switched on the ignition. For the air conditioning.

That gets up my nose, too, that sort of thing, people who don't turn off the engine when they stop somewhere just so that they can keep their feet warm or their head cool. But, anyway, never mind. We'll talk about global warming some other day. She'd locked herself away, which was something to be thankful for. Let's stay positive.

Simon stretched his legs while we got changed. I'd bought a magnificent sari in the Passage Brady right next to my house. It was turquoise, embroidered with gold thread and pearls and tiny bells. I had a little camisole, a very tight straight long skirt slit high on the thigh, and the sari like a wrap to throw over it all.

It was gorgeous.

Dangly earrings, all the amulets from Rajasthan around my neck, ten bangles on my right wrist and nearly twice that many on my left.

'You look great,' said Lola. 'Incredible. Only you could get away with something like that.

You've got such a lovely stomach, all flat and muscular.'

'Hey,' I said, feeling radiant but trying not to show it, 'six floors without a lift … '

'Having kids means you can hardly see my bellybutton any more. You'll be careful, won't you? You'll use cream every day, and—'

I shrugged. I couldn't think that far ahead.

'Can you button me up?' she chirped, turning her back to me.

Lola was wearing her black silk dress for the umpteenth time. Very sober, sleeveless, with a round neckline and a million tiny looped buttons all the way down the back.

'You haven't gone to too much expense for dear Hubert's wedding,' I said.

She turned round with a smile.

'Hey … '

'What?'

'How much do you think I paid for the hat?'

'Two hundred?'

She shrugged.

'How much?'

'I can't tell you,' she laughed, 'it's too awful.'

'Stop laughing, stupid, I can't do the buttons.'

Ballet pumps were in that year. Hers were soft, with a little bow; mine were covered in golden sequins.

Simon clapped his hands. 'C'mon, Bluebell Girls. All aboard!'

Holding tight to my sister's arm so I wouldn't stumble, I muttered, 'I warn you, if that codfish asks me whether I'm going to a fancy-dress party, I'll make her eat your hat.'

Carine didn't get a chance to say a thing because I immediately had to get up again the minute I sat down. My skirt was too tight and I had to take it off so as not to split it.

Sitting in my thong on those alpaca viscose car seats, I was … majestic.

We put on make-up using my compact while our resident echinococcosian double-checked the position of her clip-on earrings in the mirror on the sun visor.

Simon begged the three of us not to put on perfume at the same time.

We arrived in Backwater-in-the-wold in good time. Behind the car I slipped on my skirt and we went to stand outside the entrance to the church while the good folk of Backwater looked on in astonishment from their windows.

The pretty young woman in grey and pink chatting with Uncle Georges over there was our mother. We rushed over to hug her, careful not to let her get lipstick on us.

She very diplomatically kissed her daughter-in-law first, complimenting her on her outfit, and then she turned to us, laughing.

'Garance, you look superb. All that's missing is the bindi on your forehead!'

'That would take the biscuit,' blurted Carine, before turning to our poor withered uncle. 'As far as I'm aware we're not at a carnival.'

Lola made as if to hand me her hat, and we burst out laughing.

Our mother turned to Simon. 'Were they this unbearable the entire trip?'

'Even worse than that,' he said gravely.

And added: 'Where's Vincent? Isn't he with you?'

'No. He's at work.'

'What do you mean, at work?'

'Well, back at his château.'

Our elder brother shrank four inches all of a sudden.

'But ... I thought ... He told me he was coming.'

'I tried to persuade him but nothing doing. You know, Vincent and petits-fours ... '

Simon seemed devastated.

'I had a present for him. A really rare vinyl LP. Plus I really wanted to see him. I haven't seen him since Christmas. God, I'm so disappointed. I think I need a drink.'

Lola made a face.

'Caramba. Simon he no look very happy.'

'I'll say,' I muttered, glaring at Miss Spoilsport who was in the process of sucking up to all our aged aunties. 'I'll say.'

'Well, girls,' said our mother, 'you look wonderful at any rate! You'll cheer us all up, won't you, and you'll get your brother to dance this evening?'

And she moved away to dispense the usual courtesies.

We followed her with our gaze – such a tiny little woman. Graceful, charming, full of energy, elegant, so much class …

A typical Parisienne.

Lola's face clouded over. Two adorable, laughing little girls were running to join the procession.

'Right,' she said, 'I think I'll go over and join Simon.'

I stood there like an idiot in the middle of the square; the folds of my sari suddenly felt all limp.

But not for long, in fact, because our cousin Sixtine came up to me with a cackle.

'Hey, Garance! Hare Krishna! You going to a fancy-dress party or something?'

I smiled as best I could, and refrained from commenting on her poorly bleached moustache or her apple-green suit from the Christine Laure chain in Besançon.

No sooner had she moved on than it was my aunt Geneviève who renewed the attack. 'Good Lord, is that you, my little Clémence? Good God, what's that metal thing in your bellybutton? It doesn't hurt now, does it?'

Okay, I thought, I'd better go and join Simon and Lola at the café.

They were both sitting outside – their beers within reach, their heads thrown back to the sun, their legs stretched out before them.

I sat down to the sound of *cccrrrr* and ordered the same thing.

Elated, left in peace at last, our lips festooned with foam, we observed the good folk standing in their doorways observing the good folk outside the church. A feast for the eyes.

'Hey, is that Olivier's new wife – after the first one cheated on him?'

'You mean the short brunette?'

'Nah, the blonde next to the Larochaufées …'

'Help. God, she's even uglier than the first one. Get a load of that handbag.'

'A fake Gucci.'

'Exactly. Even worse than the ones those street vendors in Italy sell. Fake Goo Chee from Beijing.'

'Disgraceful.'

We could have gone on like that for ever if Carine hadn't come looking for us.

'Are you coming? It's about to start.'

'We're coming, we're coming,' said Simon. 'Let me finish my beer.'

'But if we don't go right away,' she insisted, 'we'll have lousy seats and I won't see a thing.'

'You go ahead. I'll catch you up.'

'Hurry, okay?'

She was already twenty metres away when she turned round to shout, 'Call in at that little grocery store opposite and buy some rice, will you?'

And she turned round yet again.

'Not the expensive kind, though! Don't get Uncle Ben's, like last time! It's not worth it for ...'

'Yeah, yeah,' he muttered into his beard.

We saw the bride off in the distance on her daddy's arm. A girl who, soon enough, would have a whole string of little ones with big Mickey Mouse ears. We started counting how many people were arriving late, and cheered an altar-boy who was streaking breathlessly across the square, tripping on his gown.

When the bells had fallen silent and the locals had returned to their oilcloth-covered tables, Simon said, 'I'd like to see Vincent.'

'You know, even if we call him now,' said Lola, picking up her bag, 'by the time he gets here …'

Just then a kid from the wedding party in flannel trousers with his hair parted on the side ran by. Simon called out to him.

'Hey, kid, you want to win five rounds on the pinball machine?'

'Yeah!'

'Then go back and sit through Mass and come and get us at the end of the sermon.'

'Will you give me the money right now?'

Can you believe it? Kids nowadays are just too much.

'Here you go, you little crook. And no cheating, okay? Come and get us?'

'Do I have time for a round first?'

'Yeah, go on,' sighed Simon, 'but then after that head straight into the church.'

'Okay.'

We sat on for a moment and then Simon said, 'What if we go and see him?'

'Who?'

'Vincent, of course.'

'But when?' I asked.

'Now.'

'Now?'

'You mean: now,' echoed Lola.

'Are you out of your mind? You want to take the car and go there *now*?'

'My dear Garance, I think you have just perfectly summed up what I meant to say.'

'That's crazy!' said Lola. 'We can't just get up and leave like that.'

'Why not?' (He was hunting around for change in his pocket.) 'Right. Are you girls coming?'

We didn't react. He raised his arms to the sky. 'We're out of here, I said! Come on! Let's cut and run, make ourselves scarce. Time for our great escape.'

'And what about Carine?'

He lowered his arms.

He took a pen out of his jacket and turned the beer mat over.

We have gone to visit Vincent's château. I leave Carine with you. Her things are in front of your car. Hugs.

'Hey, kid! There's been a change of plan. You don't need to go back to Mass, just give this to the lady in grey with a pink hat; her name is Maud. Got it?'

The boy nodded.

'How're you doing?'

'Two extra balls.'

'Repeat what I just said to you.'

'I get my name on the high scorers' board and after that I give your beer mat to a lady with a pink hat called Maud.'

'Keep an eye out, and give it to her when she leaves the church.'

'Okay, but it'll cost you more.'

He chuckled to himself.

'You forgot to leave the vanity case.'

'Oops. Have to go back. She would never forgive me.'

I left it out in full view on top of her bag and then we took off in a cloud of dust. As if we had just robbed a bank.

At first, no one dared say a thing. But there was this nervous, happy excitement all the same, and Simon looked in his rear view-mirror every ten seconds.

Maybe we thought we'd hear the sirens of a police car hot on our heels – compliments of Carine, rabid and foaming at the mouth. But no, not a sound. Dead calm.

Lola was sitting in the front and I leaned forward, between the two of them. We were all waiting for someone to break the awkward silence.

Simon switched on the radio; the Bee Gees were bleating, *And we're stayin' alive, stayin' alive. Ha ha ha ha … stayin' alive, stayin' alive …*

Well, what do you know. It was too good to be true. It was a sign! The hand of God! (No. It was from Pattie to Danny to celebrate the anniversary of the day they met at the dance in Treignac in 1978, but we only found that out afterwards.) We all started wailing in unison, '*HA HA HA HA! STAYIN' ALIIIIIIII-VVVVE!*' while Simon zig-zagged along the D114, yanking his tie off.

I put my jeans back on and Lola handed me her hat to put next to me on the seat.

Given what she'd paid for it, she was a bit dis-appointed.

'Hey,' I said, to try and console her, 'you can wear it at my wedding.'

Peals of laughter resounding through the little car.

We'd rescued our good mood. We'd managed to eject the alien from our spacecraft.

All we needed now was to pick up the last crew member.

I hunted on the map for the village where Vincent was living, and Lola played DJ. We could choose between France Bleu Creuse and Radio Gélinotte. Hardly the greatest sounds in the world but what did it matter? We were yacking away like crazy.

'I would never have dreamt you were capable of doing something like this,' she said at last, turning to our chauffeur.

'As you get older you get wiser,' he smiled, taking the cigarette I held out to him.

We'd been driving for two hours and I was telling them about my stay in Lisbon when I—

'What is it?' said Lola anxiously.

'Did you see that?'

'See what?'

'The dog.'

'What dog?'

'On the side of the road.'

'Dead?'

'No. Abandoned.'

'Why are you getting so worked up?'

'It's the way he looked at me, don't you see?'

They didn't see.

I was sure that dog had been looking at me.

I felt suddenly depressed, but then Lola said something about our escape and she howled the music from *Mission Impossible* at the top of her voice and I stopped thinking about the dog.

I sat there holding the map and daydreaming, thinking about those poker games last night. I had really chanced my luck, that last round with my four deuces, but what do you know ... I had won all the same.

And now it all made sense.

When we got there, the last tour of the day had just started.

A young guy, pasty-faced and pretty scruffy, with a bovine look in his eye, suggested we join the group up on the second floor.

There were a few lost-looking tourists, some women with flabby thighs, a pair of rapt school-teachers in their Birkenstocks, indifferent families, grumpy kids, and a small Dutch group. They all turned round and stared when we joined the group.

As for Vincent, he hadn't seen us yet. He had his back to us and was waffling on about his machicolations with a zeal we didn't know he had in him.

Initial shock: he was wearing a threadbare blazer, a striped shirt, cuff links, a little cravat in his collar, and a pair of dubious trousers, but with turn-ups all the same. He was close-shaven and his hair was combed back.

Second shock: the complete and utter bullshit coming from his mouth.

This château had been in the family for several generations. Nowadays, he lived there on his own while waiting to start a family and restore the moats.

The place had a curse on it because it had been built in secret for the mistress of François I's third bastard. The mistress, a certain Isaure de Haut-Brébant, had gone mad with jealousy on his account, so the legend went, and dabbled in witchcraft when the fancy took her.

'... And even today, ladies and gentlemen, on nights when the moon is orange, during the first Decan, you can hear very strange sounds, a sort of groaning, coming from the cellars, the very cellars that were used as a prison once upon a time ...

'When my grandfather was in the process of rebuilding the present-day kitchens, which you will see shortly, he discovered bones dating from the time of the Hundred Years War, and a few *écus* stamped with the seal of St Louis. On your left is a tapestry from the twelfth century, and on your right, a portrait of the famous courtesan. Notice the beauty spot beneath her left eye, irrefutable proof of some sort of divine curse ...

'Whatever you do don't miss the magnificent view from the terrace. On very windy days, you can just make out the towers of Saint-Roch ...

'This way, please. Mind the step.'

Pinch me, I must be dreaming.

The tourists stared attentively at the witch's beauty spot, and asked him whether he was ever afraid at night.

'By Jove, I have all I need to defend myself!'

With a broad sweep of his arm he took in armour, halberds, crossbows and other assorted clubs and bludgeons hanging in the stairway.

The visitors nodded gravely and cameras were raised.

What on earth was this utter lunacy?

When we walked past him as we left the room, his face lit up. Very discreetly, mind, a nod at most. The complicity of blood and long-standing affiliation.

The emblem of true Nobility.

Amidst helmets and harquebuses we fell about laughing, while he went on to enumerate the difficulties inherent in the maintenance of such a demesne ... Four hundred square metres of roofing, two kilometres of gutters, thirty rooms, fifty-two windows and twenty-five fireplaces, but — no heating. Or electricity for that matter. And no running water, now that you mention it. Whence the difficulty, for your humble servant, in finding a fiancée …

The visitors were laughing.

'… Here you have a very rare portrait of the Comte de Dunois. Notice the coat of arms, which you will also find sculpted on the pediment of the grand stairway in the northwest corner of the courtyard.

'We are now entering a bedroom with an alcove that was furnished in the eighteenth century by my great-great-grandmother the Marquise de La Lariotine, who came to hunt foxes in the region. Not only foxes, alas … And my poor uncle, the Marquis, had no cause to be jealous of the magnificent stag antlers I am sure you paused to admire in the dining room earlier on the tour … Do be careful, Madame, that is fragile. Now, I recommend you have a look in the little bathroom just here … The brushes, salt boxes and jars of ointment are all original … No, Mademoiselle, that chamber pot is from the second half of the twentieth century and that is a container for absorbing humidity …

'... Now we are coming to the most beautiful part of the château, the spiral staircase of the north wing with its superb annular barrel vault. A pure Renaissance masterpiece ...

'Please don't touch – time is hard at work, and a thousand fingertips, I am sorry to say, can do all the damage of a miner's hammer ...'

I could not believe my ears.

'Unfortunately I cannot show you the chapel, which is presently under restoration, but I beg you not to leave my modest dwelling until you have had a stroll through the grounds, where you cannot help but feel the strange vibrations coming from all these stones which, may I remind you, were brought here for the purpose of providing a refuge for the love of a man who was but a mere heartbeat from the throne, and who had been cruelly caught in the net of a wicked enchantress ...'

Murmurs in the audience.

'... For those of you who are interested, near the exit to the grounds you can have your picture taken in a suit of armour, and that is also where you will find postcards and the toilets.

'I wish you all a pleasant day. May I please remind you, ladies and gentlemen, not to forget your guide. What am I saying – guide! A poor man indentured to his estate! A privileged slave, who asks not for alms but merely a means of subsistence, until the Comte de Paris is restored to his rightful throne ...

'Thank you.

'Thank you, Mesdames.

'Dank u wel, Meneer.'

We followed the group; he disappeared through a secret door.

The willing peasants were under his spell.

We smoked a cigarette while we waited.

A guy at the entrance rigged the kids up in a dented suit of armour and took pictures of them while they brandished their weapon of choice.

Two euros per Polaroid.

'Jordan, do be careful! You're going to poke your sister's eye out!'

The guy was either totally zen, or totally stoned, or totally retarded. He moved around very slowly and deliberately and seemed to have no nerves at all. With a superstrong Gitane dangling from his lips and a Chicago Bulls baseball cap on backwards, he was a pretty weird sight. *Fantasia* meets *Forrest Gump*, sort of.

'Jordan! Put that thing down!!'

Once everyone had left, Total Retard took a rake and shuffled off, chewing on his fag.

We were beginning to wonder whether the little Baron de La Lariotine would ever deign to grace us with his presence.

I couldn't stop saying, 'Pinch me … Can you believe this? … What the …?' and shaking my head.

Simon was fascinated by the mechanism of the drawbridge, and Lola set about rearranging a rambling rose.

Vincent emerged at last, with a smile. He was wearing a worn pair of jeans and a Sundyata T-shirt.

'Hey! What the fuck are you all doing here?'
'We missed you.'
'Really? That's cool.'

'How're things?'

'Great. Aren't you supposed to be at Hubert's wedding?'

'Yeah, but we got lost on the way.'

'I see … great.'

That was him all over. Calm, lovely. Not making a big deal out of seeing us there, but really happy all the same.

A moonstruck Pierrot, a Martian, our little brother, our very own Vincent.

It was cool.

'So,' he said, spreading his arms, 'what do you think of my little campsite?'

'Yeah, what the hell do you mean spouting rubbish like that?'

'What? You mean the stuff I tell people? Oh … it's not all rubbish. She really existed, this Isaure, it's just that … Well, I can't be sure she came this way. According to the archives, she's actually from the dump down the road but since their château burned down, down the road … We had to find her somewhere to live, didn't we?'

'Yeah, but what about all that palaver, about ancestors and dressing up like an impoverished toff, and all the fairy tales you were telling them just now?'

'Oh, that? Put yourselves in my place. I got here at the beginning of May to work the season. The old biddy told me she was going off on her spa treatment and she'd pay me the first month when she got back. Since then, not a word. She's vanished. It's already August and I haven't had a penny. No lady of the manor, no pay slip or money order, *nada*. I've got to live off something, haven't I? That's why I had to make up that whole shtick. All I've got to live on is the tips, and you can't get tips just like that. People want their money's worth and as you can see it's not exactly Disneyland here. So I get out the blazer and the signet ring, and head straight for the battlements.'

'Unbelievable.'

'Lady, a man's gotta do what a man's gotta do.'

'And who's the other guy?'

'That's Nono. He gets paid by the village council.'

'And uh, isn't he – does he have all his marbles?'

Vincent finished rolling his cigarette, then said, 'I don't really know. All I know is that he's Nono. If you understand Nono, that's fine, otherwise it's hard going.'

'But what do you do all day?'

'In the morning I sleep, in the afternoon I lead the tours, and the evening is for my music.'

'Here?'

'In the chapel. I'll show you. And what about you guys? What are you up to?'

'Well, we, uh … not much. We wanted to take you out for dinner.'

'When? Tonight?'

'Well, yeah, obviously. Not after the next Crusades.'

'Nah, tonight's no good. Nono's niece is getting married, and I'm invited.'

'Hey! Just let us know if we're in the way, won't you?'

'You're not, not at all! It's really great you're here. We'll work something out. Nono!'

Nono turned round, slowly.

'Do you think it would be a problem if my brother and sisters came along this evening?'

Nono stared at us for the longest time, then said, 'He's your brother?'

'Yeah.'

'And they're your sisters?'

'Yes.'

'They still virgins?'

'Hey, Nono, that's not what I asked you! Shit, Nono. Do you think they can come tonight?'

'Who?'

'Oh, fuck, this guy's driving me crazy – my brother and sisters!'

'Come where?'

'To Sandy's wedding!'

Nono pointed his chin towards me and said, 'Will she be coming, too?'

Gulp.

Why do I get stuck with the horrible Gollum?

Vincent slumped in despair.

'He drives me crazy. Just recently, I don't know how he did it, there was this kid who got stuck in the suit of armour and we had to call the fire brigade. What are you laughing about? You're not the ones who have to deal with him every day, are you?'

'So why are you going to his niece's wedding, then?'

'I have no choice. He's really sensitive, you know. Yeah, yeah, go ahead and laugh, my lady virgins. Say, Simon, they haven't changed, these two, have they? Besides, his mother gives me loads of really good stuff. Terrines, vegetables from her garden, salami … If it weren't for her, I wouldn't survive.'

I could not believe my ears.

'Anyway, this is all very well, but I've got to count up the money in the till, clean the toilets, help the retard rake the walks and lock all the doors.'

'How many are there?'

'Eighty-four.'

'We'll help.'

'Okay, great. There's a rake over there, and for the toilets, you'll need the hose.'

We rolled up the sleeves of our fine apparel and got to work.

'I think we're done now. Do you want to go for a swim?'

'Where?'

'There's a stream, down there.'

'Is it clean?' asked Lola.

'You sure the foxes don't piss in it?' I added.

'Sorry?'

We weren't too keen.

'Are you going?'

'I go every evening.'

'Okay, we're coming.'

Simon and Vincent were walking ahead.

'I've got an MC5 album on vinyl for you.'

'No, really?'

'Yeah.'

'First pressing?'

'Yup.'

'Cool. How did you find it?'

'Well, you know, nothing's too good for our lord and master.'

'You coming for a swim?'

'Of course.'

'Hey, girls! You coming for a swim?'

'No way, not while that maniac is anywhere near,' I murmured to Lola.

'No, we'll just watch!'

'He's around here somewhere,' I muttered, clenching my teeth. 'I can feel it. He's staring at us, from behind the bushes.'

My sister just laughed.

Lola pulled the trashy magazine from my bag and looked up our horoscope.

'You're Aquarius, aren't you?'

'Huh? What?' I went, turning round abruptly to scare off Nono the onanist.

'Right ... are you listening?'

'Yes.'

'*Be on your guard. Venus is in Leo; anything can happen. An encounter, True Love, the one you are waiting for is close at hand. Make the most of your charm and sex appeal and, above all, leave yourself open to chance. Your strong character has played tricks on you in the past. Time to indulge in some romantic sentiment.*'

She was killing herself laughing, the idiot.

'Nono! Come back! She's here! She wants to indulge in some roman—'

I put my hand over her mouth.

'Would you shut up? I'm sure you just made it all up.'

'I didn't! Here, look if you don't believe me!'

98

I tore the rag from her hands.

'Show me—'

'There, look … *Venus is in Leo*, I'm not making it up.'

'What garbage.'

'Well, if I were you, I'd be on my guard all the same.'

'Tsk. This is all bullshit.'

'You're right. Let's have a look and see who's been prancing around Saint-Tropez.'

'Hang on. You're not telling me those breasts are real?'

'Precisely, I'm not telling you that.'

'And have you seen the— Heeey! Simon, get out of here or I'm calling your wife!'

Like two dogs, the boys were shaking themselves gleefully, showering us with icy water.

We should have seen it coming. Or remembered, rather. Vincent's cheeks were full of water and he started chasing after Lola, who ran across the field screaming, popping all the buttons off her dress.

I hurried to pick up all our things and went to join them, spitting *pssht!* and *out!* at every bush I went past, making the sign of snail's horns with my index and little fingers.

Begone, Beelzebub!

Vincent took us on a tour of his private quarters in the servants' wing. Basic.

He had brought a bed down from the second floor – where it was too warm for him – and taken up residence in the stables. And what do you know, he'd chosen the box that had belonged to Lover Boy.

Between Polka and Hurricane.

He'd done himself up like a lord. Boots impeccably polished. A pure white 1970s suit. Hipsters and a pale-pink silk shirt with a collar so pointy that it reached the armholes. On anyone else it would have looked ridiculous, but on Vincent it was as classy as it gets.

He went to grab his guitar. Simon took the wedding gift from the boot of the car and we headed down to the village.

The evening light was sublime. The whole countryside was ochre, bronze and old gold, resting after a long day. Vincent told us to turn round and admire his castle.

It was splendid.

'You're teasing me.'

'We're not, really,' said Lola, always mindful of Universal Harmony.

Simon began to sing, 'I'm the king of the caaaastle, and you're the dirty raaaascals.'

Simon was singing, Vincent was laughing, and Lola was smiling. All four of us were walking along a warm pavement leading into a little village in Indre.

There was a faint smell of tar, mint and freshly mown hay in the air. The cows gazed at us admiringly and the birds called to each other, time for dinner.

A beautiful moment in time.

Lola and I had put our hats and various disguises back on.

No reason not to: a wedding is a wedding.

Or, at least that is what we told ourselves, until we arrived at our destination.

We entered an overheated parish hall that smelled of sweat and old socks. Tatami mats were piled high in one corner and the bride was sitting under a basketball hoop. She looked as if she didn't know what had hit her.

The tables were laid out for a banquet worthy of Astérix, with local plonk in a box and old favourites blasting out at full volume.

A huge lady decked out with ruffles hurried over to our little brother.

'Ah! Here he is! Come here, son, follow me! Nono said you had family with you. All of you, follow me, come on! Just look at you all; you look grand! What a hat! And what a slip of a girl this one is! You're so thin – don't they feed you in Paris? Have a seat. Have something to eat, children. Eat whatever you want. There's plenty. Just ask Gérard to get you something to drink. Gérard! Come over here, lad!'

Vincent couldn't extricate himself from her hugs and kisses; I stood there comparing. What a difference between this woman, a complete stranger, and the polite disdain of my great-aunts just a few hours ago. I couldn't believe my eyes.

'Do you think maybe we should go and congratulate the bride?'

'Go right ahead,' said the huge lady, 'and see if you can't find Gérard on the way. Unless he's already under the table – that wouldn't look good now, would it?'

'What's the present?' I asked Simon.
He didn't know.

We kissed the bride, one after the other.
The groom was as red as a lobster. He was looking sceptically at the gift his bride had just unwrapped: a superb cheese plate, carefully chosen by Carine. It was an oval thing with handles made of vine stock and vine leaves sculpted in Plexiglas.
I don't think he was altogether convinced.

We sat down at the end of a table, and two old guys who were already pretty far gone welcomed us with open arms.

'Gé-rard! Gé-rard! Gé-rard! Hey, kids! Go and get some food for our friends. Gérard! Where the hell has he got to?'

Gérard arrived with his boxed wine and the party began.

After mixed veg in mayonnaise on a scallop shell, and grilled lamb with French fries à la mayonnaise, and goat's cheese, and three slices of wedding cake, everyone moved back to make room for Guy Macroux and his *orchestre de charme*.

We felt blessed. Ears flapping, eyes wide open, taking everything in. On our right was the bride, opening the dance with her dad, to an air by Strauss on the squeeze box, and to our left were the old guys, noisily crossing swords over the new one-way sign in front of the Pidoune bakery.

It was all so picturesque.

No. I can put it better than that, and less condescendingly: it was a moment to savour.

Guy Macroux had something of Dario Moreno about him.

Little dyed moustache, a flamboyant jacket, expensive bling and a velvety voice.

With the first bars of the accordion, everyone flocked to the dance floor.

Pdum pdum pdum, just a little chachacha
Ah!
Pdum pdum pdum, step to the mambo
Oh!

'C'mon, all together now!'
La la la la … la la la la …
'I can't hear you!'
LA LA LA LA … LA LA LA LA …

'And at the back, there! Come on grannies! Sing along, girls!'
Opidibi poi poi!

Lola and I went wild, and I had to roll up my skirt to keep the rhythm.

The boys, as usual, weren't dancing. Vincent was chatting up a young lady with a milky white cleavage, and Simon was listening to some old timer's mildewed memories.

Then we had, *Gar-ter! Gar-ter! Gar-ter!* where things got a little steamed up and there was a lot of joking about big sausages. The young bride was wheelbarrowed onto a table-tennis table and … well, it's not really worth going into. Or maybe it's just me, maybe I'm too squeamish.

I went outside. I was beginning to miss Paris.

Lola came to join me for 'ze moonlight cigarette'.

This guy followed her out, his matted body hair gleaming with sweat. He just had to ask her to dance again.

He was wearing a Hawaiian shirt, viscose trousers, white socks with a tennis stripe, and woven loafers.

Irresistibly charming.

And, and, and – I almost forgot: one of those black leather photographer's vests! Three pockets on the left and two on the right. And a penknife in his belt. And a mobile phone in a case. And an earring. And dark glasses. And a chain attached to his wallet. All that was missing was the whip.

Indiana Jones in person.

'You going to introduce me?'

'Uh, yes, this is my sister Garance, and uh—'

'You've forgotten my name already?'

'Uh ... Jean-Pierre?'

'Michel.'

'Oh, yes, Michel! Michel Garance, Garance Michel ... '

'Hi,' I said, as sternly as possible.

'Jean-Michel. My name is Jean-Michel. Jean like John and Michel like Mont-Saint-Michel, but hey, I won't hold it against you. Cheers! So you're sisters, eh? It's weird, you don't look at all alike. Are you sure one of you didn't come in the post?'

Ha. Ha. Ha.

Once he'd moved away, Lola shook her head.

'God, I couldn't take it any more, how did I get stuck with the biggest creep in the county? Did you note his refined sense of humour? Even *Blankety Blank* wouldn't have had him. The guy is a disaster.'

'Shush, he's coming back.'

'Hey! Have you heard the one about the guy with five dicks?'

'Uh … no. Haven't had that pleasure.'

'So there's this guy. He's got five dicks.'

Silence.

'So?' I ask.

'So his pants fit him like a glove!'

Help.

'And the one about the tart who wouldn't give head?'

'Sorry?'

'Do you know what men call a tart who won't give head?'

More than anything, it was my sister's expression that made me want to laugh. My sister, always so classy with her vintage Saint Laurent, her ballet school gracefulness, her intaglio ring and the way she could get all flustered just eating off a paper tablecloth. So with her flabbergasted air and her eyes as big as Sèvres bisque saucers, it was glorious.

'Well?'

'Sorry, no. I give up, too. What do you call a call girl who, er—'

(Classy *and* funny. I adore her.)

'Well, they don't call her! Ha! Ha! Ha!'

He was on a roll, now … He spun round to face me, his thumbs hooked in the pockets of his waistcoat.

'And you? Have you heard the one about the guy who wrapped his hamster in duct tape?'

'No. But I don't want you to tell it because it's too disgusting.'

'Oh, yeah? So you have heard it?'

'Uh, look, Jean-Montsaintmichel, I need to have a few words with my sister, here.'

'Okay, okay, I'll go. So, anyway, see ya later, pussycats!'

'Is he gone? Really truly gone?'

'Yes, but Toto is coming to take his place.'

'Who's Toto?'

Nono sat down on a chair facing us.

He was looking at us, whilst diligently scratching the inside of his trouser pockets.

Right.

Probably it was his brand-new suit; must have been causing him some local itching.

Saint Lola gave him a faint smile to put him at ease.

Of the type: Hiya Nono. We're your new friends! Welcome to our heart.

'Are you still virgins?' he asked.

Did he have a bee in his bonnet or what?! (No way!)

Our Singing Nun kept her cool: 'So, you're the caretaker over at the château, aren't you?'

'Hey, you shut up. I'm talking to her, the one with the big tits.'

I knew it. Yes, I knew it.

Someday we'll all laugh about it. Someday we'll be old and grey and since we won't have done our pelvic floor exercises the way we should, we'll wet ourselves when we look back on that day. But at the time, it didn't make me laugh at all because ... because Nono was drooling a little bit out of the side of his mouth where he didn't have his cigarette butt, and it really freaked me out. The thin thread of saliva that just kept coming, in the moonlight.

Thank God, Simon and Vincent showed up just then.

'Shall we be off?'

'Good idea.'

'I'll catch up with you, I just have to pick up my guitar.'

All the love I have for you-ou-ou
Wap doo wa dowa dowa … Wap doo wa …

Guy Macroux's voice echoed through the village streets. We danced our way through the parked cars.

My cries of joy-oy-oy, they're thanks to you-ou-ou

'Where are you taking us?'

Vincent was circling the château, heading down a dark path.

'Let's have one last drink. A nightcap if you like. Are you tired, girls?'

'What about Nono? Is he following us?'

'Of course not. Forget about him. Are you coming?'

It was a gypsy camp. There were twenty caravans or so, each one bigger than the previous one, and there were big white vans, laundry, duvets, bicycles, kids, washbasins, tyres, satellite dishes, TVs, cooking pots, dogs, hens, and even a little black piglet.

Lola was horrified.

'It's after midnight and these kids aren't in bed. Poor things.'

Vincent laughed.

'Do you think they look unhappy or something?'

The kids were laughing, running all over the place; they rushed up to Vincent. They fought over who would carry his guitar, and the little girls took us by the hand.

They were fascinated by my bangles.

'They're on their way to Saintes-Maries-de-la-Mer. I hope they'll be gone by the time the old biddy comes back, because I'm the one who told them they could stay here.'

'Just like Captain Haddock in *The Castafiore Emerald*,' laughed Simon.

An old man took Vincent in his arms.

'Hey, son, here you are.'

He'd certainly found himself a few families, our little Vincent. It was hardly surprising he'd snubbed ours.

And then it was straight out of an old Kusturica film, from before he got bigheaded.

The old guys were singing these songs that were so sad you could weep – it just turned you inside out – and the young ones were clapping their hands while the women danced round the fire. Most of them were fat and badly dressed but when they moved, even the air around them seemed to be in motion.

The kids were still running all over the place and the grannies were watching television and rocking the babies to sleep. Almost all of them had gold teeth and they smiled proudly to make sure we knew it.

Vincent was right at home with them, happy as Larry. He played his guitar; his eyes were closed, maybe just concentrating a fraction more than usual, so he could keep the tune and a certain distance.

The old men had fingernails like talons and the wood on the fret boards of their guitars was all worn down beneath the strings.

Gling gling, toc.

Even if you didn't understand the words, it wouldn't be hard to guess the lyrics.

Where are you, my country? Oh where are you, my love?
Oh where are you, my friend? Oh where are you, my son?

And it went on to say, more or less,

I have no more country, only memories now.
My love is gone, only heartache now.
I've lost my friend, this song is for him.

An old woman brought us some flat beer. The minute we finished our glasses she came back with more.

Lola's eyes were shining; she was sitting with two kids on her lap, rubbing her chin on their hair. Simon looked at me with a smile.

We had come a long way, the two of us, since this morning.

Oops, here came the irrepressible old granny with her lukewarm watery lager.

I motioned to Vincent to ask him if he had something to smoke, but his answer was along the lines of hush, later. This was a new twist on things. Here we were among these good folk who don't send their kids to school, and there might well be a little Mozart rotting away in this dump of theirs, and they do what they like with the laws we hard-working sedentary folk come up with, but they don't smoke weed.

By all the saints of Merco-Benz, we'll have none of that here.

'You girls take Isaure's bed.'

'With all that moaning from the dungeon? No thanks.'

'But I was making all that up!'

'And with that maniac who has a set of keys? No way. We're sleeping in here with you!'

'All right, calm down, Garance.'

'Don't tell me to calm down! I'm still a virgin and I'd like to stay that way!'

I was dead tired, but I still managed to get a laugh out of them. I was actually rather proud of myself.

The boys slept in Lover Boy's stall, and we curled up in Hurricane's.

Simon woke us. He'd been down to the village for croissants.

'From Pidoule's?' I asked with a yawn.

'From Pidoune's.'

Vincent didn't open the gates that day.

Closed due to rock fall, he wrote on a piece of cardboard.

He showed us around the chapel. He and Nono had moved the château's piano up to the altar so now all the angels in heaven could swing along.

We were treated to a little concert.

There we were, on a Sunday morning, sitting in a pew. Well-mannered and contemplative in the light of the stained glass, listening to a new version of knock, knock, knockin' on heaven's door …

Lola wanted to visit every nook and cranny of the château. I asked Vincent to give us a rerun of his show. We were in stitches.

He showed us everything: the chatelaine's chambers, her girdles, her commode, her coypu traps, her recipes for coypu pâté, her bottle of eau-de-vie and her old guide to the *Peerage, Baronetage and Knightage*, all greasy from so much fingering. And then the cellars, the wines, the outbuildings, the saddle room, the hunting lodge and the old rampart walk.

Simon was amazed by the ingeniousness of the architects and other fortress-building experts. Lola was herb-gathering.

I sat down on a stone bench and observed the three of them.

My brothers leaning over the moat ... Simon must be missing his latest remote-controlled model. Oh if only See-sull Dabbleyou could see him now. Vincent must have read his mind, because he said, 'Forget about your little boats. There are humongous carp in there. They'd chew them up in no time.'

'Are you serious?'

A dreamy silence, to stroke the lichen on the parapet ...

'Actually, you know what,' murmured our Captain Ahab eventually, 'it would be much more entertaining. I'll have to come back with Léo. Just to see some huge sub-moatian monster swallow down those precious toys he's never been allowed to go near – might be the best thing that could ever happen to the two of us.'

I didn't hear what he said after that but I could see they were high-fiving as if they'd just made a really good deal.

And there was my Lola, on her knees with her sketchbook among the daisies and the sweet peas. My sister's back, a few daring white butterflies, her hair held up by a paintbrush, her long neck, her arms emaciated by the recent divorce, the bottom of her T-shirt crumpled as she used it to smudge her paint. A palette of white cotton that gradually took on its own colours ...

I have never been more sorry not to have my camera with me.

Let's just chalk it up to fatigue, but I found myself wallowing in sentimentality. A huge wave of tenderness washed over me looking at the three of them: somehow this felt like the last magic show, the last birthday party of our childhood.

For almost thirty years they'd been making my life a place of beauty. What would I become without them? When would life decide it was time for us to part?

For that's the way it goes. For time parts those who love one another, and nothing lasts.

What we were experiencing at that moment – something all four of us were aware of – was a windfall. Borrowed time, an interlude, a moment of grace. A few hours stolen from other people.

How much longer would we have the strength to tear ourselves away from everyday life and resist? How often would life give us the chance to play truant? To thumb our noses at it? Or make a little bit on the side? When would we lose one another, and in what way would the ties be stretched beyond repair?

How much longer before we became too old?

And I know we were all aware of this. I know what we're like.

We were too shy to talk about it, but at that precise moment on our journey, we knew.

We knew that in the shadow of that ruined castle we were living the last hours of an era, and the time for change was drawing near. Time to part with closeness and tenderness, with our rough-and-tumble love for each other. Time to let go; open our palms and grow up, at last.

Time for the Dalton Gang to go their separate ways and ride off into the sunset.

I'm such an idiot. I'd almost worked myself up into a state of solitary weeping when I saw something by the side of the path.

What was that thing?

I stood up, squinting.

An animal, a little creature was struggling to make its way towards me.

Was it hurt? What was it?

A fox?

A fox with its jar of urine sent by Carine?

A rabbit?

It was a dog.

Unbelievable.

It was the dog I'd seen from the car yesterday, the one who'd dissolved in the rear-view mirror.

It was the dog whose eyes had met mine a hundred kilometres from here.

No. It couldn't be him. But it was.

Hey, at this rate, they'd want me on Animal Planet!

I knelt down and held out my hand. He didn't even have the strength left to wag his tail. He took three more steps and collapsed at my feet.

For a few seconds I didn't move. I was scared witless.

A dog had just come to die at my feet.

But then he gave a heartbreaking little whimper, trying to lick his paw. He was bleeding.

Lola came over and said, 'Where'd this dog come from?'
I looked up at her and answered tonelessly, 'I cannot believe my eyes.'

Now the four of us gathered round to see what he needed. Vincent went to fetch some water, Lola to find some food, and Simon stole a cushion from the yellow salon.
The dog gulped down the water then collapsed in the dust. We carried him into the shade.

It was downright weird.

We put together a picnic and went down to the river.
My throat was tight at the thought that the dog would probably be history by the time we came back up. But, well … At least he'd chosen a beautiful spot for it. And he'd have fantastic mourners.

The boys wedged the bottles in the stones at the edge of the river while we spread a blanket. We had just sat down when Vincent said, 'Hey, look, there he is.'

The dog dragged himself over to me once again. He curled up against my thigh and fell asleep straight away.

'I think he's trying to tell you something,' said Simon.

All three of them were laughing, teasing me. 'Don't make such a face Garance. He loves you, that's all. Come on ... Say cheese. It's no big deal.'

'But what the hell am I supposed to do with a dog? Can you see me in my tiny studio on the seventh floor with a dog?'

'There's nothing you can do about it,' said Lola. 'Remember your horoscope? You've got Venus in Leo and you just have to accept it. This is the important encounter you had to prepare yourself for. I warned you.'

They were laughing more than ever.

'Consider it a sign from fate,' said Simon; 'this dog has come to save you—'

'– so that you'll lead a healthier, more-balanced lifestyle—' added Lola.

'– and get up in the morning to take him out for a wee,' said Simon. 'You'll have to buy a track suit and take him jogging in the country every week-end.'

'This way you'll schedule your day, and you'll feel responsible,' Vincent chimed in.

I was flabbergasted.

'Not the track suit, spare me.'

Vincent uncorked a bottle and said, 'And, any-way, he's gorgeous.'

Damn it, who could argue with that? He had bald spots and fleas and scabs, he was scruffy and ragged and mongrelly, but he was gorgeous all right.

'Seeing he's made this huge effort to find you, you're not about to abandon him now, I hope?'

I leaned over to look at him. He was pretty smelly, for one thing ...

'Will you take him to the SPA?'

'Hey! Why me? We found him all together, may I remind you!'

'Look!' shouted Lola. 'He's smiling at you.'

Shit. He was, too. He'd turned over and he was wagging his tail, limply, and he raised his eyes to look at me.

Oh … Why? Why me? Would he even fit in the basket on my bike? And my concierge had it in for me, as it was.

And what does a dog eat?

And how long does it live?

And what about that little shovel for picking up the dog mess? And the retractable lead, and the inane conversations with all the neighbours out walking their mutts after the evening film on TV, fellow members of the pooper scooper brigade?

Heaven help us.

The Bourgueil was nicely chilled. We nibbled on some *rillons* and spread rillettes in thick layers on our bread, and slowly savoured some warm, sweet tomatoes, pyramids of ashy goat's cheese, and orchard pears.

How good it felt. The water gurgling, the wind in the trees and the chatter of birds. The sun glistened on the river, shooting sparks here, vanishing there, bursting against the clouds or running along the river banks. My dog was dreaming of Paris pavements, grunting with happiness, and the flies pestered us.

We talked about the same things we'd talked about at the age of ten, or fifteen, or twenty: the books we'd read, the films we'd seen, the music we'd heard and the places we'd discovered. We talked about the Gallica online library and all the other treasures you could find on the Internet, and about the musicians we loved, and about the train or concert tickets, or the time off we dreamt of treating ourselves to, and the exhibitions we were bound to miss, and our friends and the friends of our friends and the love stories we had – or hadn't – played a part in. Mostly hadn't, as it happened, and that's when we were at our best. At telling the stories, I mean. Stretched out in the grass, devoured by all sorts of little insects, we teased each other and mocked our own selves, writhing with laughter and sunburn be damned.

And then we talked about our parents. The way we always did. About Maman and Pop. Their new lives. Their own love stories. And our future.

In short, the everyday trifles and the handful of people that filled our lives.

It wasn't much, nor many people … and yet it was everything.

Simon and Lola talked about their children. Getting on at school, mischief, the things they said which they should have written down somewhere so as not to forget them. Vincent talked at length about his music: should he go on with it? Where? How? With whom? And how much could he allow himself to hope? I told them about my new flatmate who, yes, was legal this time, and my job, and how I wasn't at all sure I was cut out to be a judge. So many years spent studying and so little self-confidence at the other end; it was disconcerting.

Had I missed a vital turning point? Where had I slipped up? And was there someone waiting for me somewhere? The other three encouraged me and gave me a kick up the backside so I pretended to go along with their kind words.

Anyway, we were all a bit shaken up, and we were all pretending to go along with the mood.

Because wasn't life a bit of a bluff, after all?

When the stack is too short and there are chips missing. When you've been dealt a terrible hand and you can't keep up ... That much we all agreed on, the four of us, with our grand dreams and our rents to be paid on the 5th of every month.

So we opened another bottle: Dutch courage.

Vincent made us laugh with his latest romantic fiasco.

'Hey, put yourselves in my shoes! There's this girl I've been after for two months. I wait for her for six hours outside her department at the university, then I invite her out to eat, three times, and take her back to her student dorm in the middle of nowhere a dozen times, and I invite her to the opera, a hundred and ten euros a shot! Shit!'

'And nothing's happened?'

'Nothing. *Nada*. Diddly-squat. Shit! Two hundred and twenty euros! Can you imagine how many records I could have bought with that?'

'Well, may I point out that a guy who counts the pennies like that deserves what he gets,' scolded Lola.

'But did you – did you even try and kiss her?' I asked naïvely.

'No. I didn't dare. That's what so stupid.'

A chorus of mocking.

'I know. I'm shy, it's stupid.'

'What's her name?'

'Eva.'

'Where's she from?'

'Dunno. She told me, but I didn't understand.'

'I see. And, uh … do you think you're in with a chance, or not?'

'Hard to say. But she showed me photos of her mother.'

That was too much.

We rolled around in the grass while Don Juan tried to pelt us with pebbles.

'Oh,' I begged, 'can I have that one?'

Lola tore a page out of her sketchbook and handed it to me, raising her eyes to heaven.

She at least had been able to see the true nobility of that heroic mutt of mine as he languished in the sun. The only male, now that I think of it, who has ever pursued me with such constancy.

The next drawing was a very pretty view of the château.

'From the English garden,' nodded Vincent.

'We should send it to Pop and write a little note,' suggested Lola.

(Our father didn't have a mobile.) (Come to think of it, he'd never had a landline either.)

Like all her other ideas from time immemorial, it was a good one, and as always and for all time, we fell in behind our elder sister.

It was as if we were at the back of the bus on our way home from summer camp. Paper and pen going from hand to hand. Thoughts, greetings, tenderness, mischief, little hearts and the big kisses that went with them.

The snag – but that wasn't our father's fault, it was May '68's – was that we didn't exactly know where to send our letter.

'I think he's working at a naval shipyard in Brighton …'

'Hardly,' joked Vincent, 'it's too cold for him there! He's got rheumatism these days, after all, he's old now! He's in Valence with Richard Lodge.'

'Are you sure?' I was surprised. 'The last time I heard from him he was on his way to Marseille.'

Silence.

'Okay,' decided Lola, 'I'll keep it in my bag for now and the first one to hear anything gets in touch with me.'

Silence.

But Vincent strummed a few chords so that we wouldn't hear it.

In her bag …

All those kisses, still stifled. All those hearts locked up along with keys and chequebooks.

But under all those cobblestones hurled in youthful rebellion, there was nothing.

Luckily for me I had my dog. He was covered with fleas and was conscientiously licking his balls.

'Why are you smiling, Garance?' asked Simon, to conceal the moment of sadness.

'Nothing. Just thinking how lucky I am.'

My sister got her paints back out, the boys had a swim and I watched my sweetheart gradually come back to life as I handed him pieces of bread smeared with *rillettes*.

He spat the bread back out, the filthy cur.

'What are you going to call him?'

'I don't know.'

Lola was the one who said it was time to leave. She didn't want to be late because of the handing over of the children, and you could already tell she was getting nervous. Worse than nervous, in fact: worried, brittle, her smile gone all crooked.

Vincent gave me back my iPod that he'd nicked months earlier.

'Here you go, like I promised ages ago, I've downloaded all the—'

'Oh, thanks! You've put on all the stuff I like?'

'No. Not everything. How could I? But you'll see, it's a good selection.'

We kissed Vincent goodbye, exchanging wise-cracks to lighten the mood, before getting into the car. Simon had already driven across the moat before he slowed down. I leaned out of the window to shout, 'Hey! Lover Boy!'

'What?'

'I've got a present for you, too!'

'What is it?'

'Eva!'

'What d'you mean, Eva?'

'She's arriving the day after tomorrow on the bus from Tours.'

He was running after us.

'Huh? What are you on about?'

'It's true! We called her just now while you were swimming.'

'Liars.' (He was white as a sheet.) 'How did you get her number, for a start?'

'We looked in the contacts on your phone.'

'It's not true.'

'You're right. It's not true. But go to the bus stop anyway, just in case.'

He was all red.

'What the hell did you tell her?'

'That you lived in a huge château and that you'd written a beautiful solo for her and she had to hear it because you'd play it for her in a chapel and it would be really *romantichno*.'

'What?'

'It's Serbo-Croat.'

'I don't believe you.'

'Too bad for you, then. Let Nono take care of her.'

'Is it true, Simon?'

'I have no idea, but knowing these two harpies, anything is possible.'

He was bright pink.

'Are you serious? The day after tomorrow?'

Simon started the car again.

'The bus at 6.40 p.m.!' said Lola.

'Across from Pidoule's!' I shouted, over her shoulder.

When he had completely disappeared from the rear view-mirror, Simon said, 'Garance?'

'What?'

'Pidou-ne.'

'Oh yeah, sorry. Look, there's that pervert! Squash him!'

We were going to wait until we were on the motorway to listen to Vincent's present.

Lola decided at last to ask Simon whether he was happy.

'Are you asking me because of Carine?'

'Sort of.'

'You know … She's much nicer at home. It's when you guys are around that she's a pain. I think she's jealous. She's afraid of you. She thinks I love you more than her and … and then, you stand for everything she is not. Your crazy side completely throws her. That *Demoiselles de Rochefort* side. She's got her hang-ups. She's got the impression that for you two life is like some huge school playground and you're the popular girls who used to tease her because she was top of the class. Those beautiful, inseparable, funny sorts of girls who she secretly admired.'

'If she only knew,' said Lola, putting her head against the window.

'But that's the thing, she doesn't know. When she's around you she feels completely lost. I know she can be a pain, but it's a good job I have her. She encourages me, motivates me, she forces me to do things. Without her I'd still be stuck with my curves and equations, that's a fact. Without her I'd be in some studio flat somewhere ruminating about quantum mechanics!'

He fell silent.

'And she has given me two beautiful presents, after all.'

As soon as we'd gone through the *péage*, I plugged the iPod into the car radio.

'So, matey, what have you got for us here?'

Trusting smiles. Simon tugged on his seatbelt to leave some room for the musicians. Lola reclined her seat and I nestled up against her shoulder.

Marvin as ringleader: *Here, My Dear … This album is dedicated to you …* A wild version of Miriam Makeba's 'Pata Pata', to loosen our joints; 'Hungry Heart' by the Boss because we'd been shaking our booties for fifteen years to that one; and further down the playlist, 'The River', to feed our hungry hearts. Then 'Beat It' by the late King of Pop, on full volume just long enough to slalom between the white lines. 'Friday I'm in Love' by The Cure in order to – hang on, let me turn the sound down – greet this fine weekend; 'Common People' by Pulp, a song that taught us more English than all our teachers put together. Then there was Boby Lapointe bemoaning the fact that *you're prettier than ever … except your heart. Your heart has lost that warmth I loved …* His 'Maman des poissons' and Eddy Mitchell's:

Maman, I'm just fourteen I promise to earn lots of money for you. A sublime version of 'I Will Survive' by Musica Nuda and another completely cracked version of 'My Funny Valentine' by Angela McCluskey. And then another one of hers, 'Don't Explain', that was enough to make the most hardened womaniser weep... Christophe in his satin waistcoat: *C'etait la dolce vita*... Yo-Yo Ma's cello for Ennio Morricone and his Jesuits. Dylan saying over and over *I want you* to two sisters who are practically virgins. *Zaza, you stink, but I love you all the same*... And what wouldn't I give to jump onto Thomas Fersen's knee... and into his suitcase too... *Let's go where destiny takes us, Germaine, let's do as we please ... Love me or leave me,* begs Nina Simone, and I'm surprised to see Lola rubbing her nose ... Vincent doesn't like to see his sister unhappy so he has thrown in a Goldman penny whistle number to cheer her up: *That's how love is and there's nothing we can do...* Montand remembering Paulette, and Bashung remembering Bashung...*hour by hour, the beekeeper is dying...* 'La Mariée' by Patachou and 'Le Petit Bal Perdu' by that old faux-naïf. Björk wailing that it's oh so quiet; Vivaldi's 'Nisi Dominus' for

137

Camille's sake, and the Neil Hannon song that Mathilde was crazy about. Kathleen Ferrier for Mahler, Glenn Gould for Bach, and Rostropovich for peace. *Une chanson douce* by Henri Salvador, the one our mother would sing to us, which we'd fall asleep to, sucking our thumbs. Dalida: *he was just eighteen, and beyoootiful as a child...* The soundtrack of *Not on the Lips*, the film coming along just when I wasn't sure I wanted to hang around too much longer. Then a pause for the weather report, the rain in Nantes from Barbara and then Luis Mariano yodelling about the sun in Mexico. Pyeng Threadgill sang 'Close to Me', and I said to myself, that's it exactly, my darlings. Cole Porter's elegance made even more sublime by Ella Fitzgerald, then some Cyndi Lauper for contrast. *Girls just wanna have fu-un!* I shout, shaking my dog like a cheerleader's pompom, and all his fleas start dancing the Macarena.

And so many others. A whole heap of delights.

Nods to the past and memories, all those greasy slow tracks in memory of rubbish parties, *music was my first looove* (for connoisseurs only!), Klezmer, Motown, old dance-hall stuff, Gregorian chant, marching bands and grand organs and then suddenly, while the car was gulping and the pump clicked madly, Léo Ferré and Louis Aragon sang out in protest, *Is this how man lives?*

The more tracks I heard, the harder it was to hold back my tears. So all right, I was tired, but I could feel this knot growing and growing at the back of my throat.

Too much emotion all at once. Simon and Lola and Vincent and Pinchme on my lap and all this music that had been my life support for so long …

I had to blow my nose.

When the iPod fell silent I thought I'd feel better, but then that bastard Vincent's voice came through the loudspeakers.

'That's it. That's all for now, pop pickers. Anyway, I hope I haven't forgotten anything … Hang on, yes, here's one for the road.'

Jeff Buckley's cover of Leonard Cohen's 'Hallelujah'.

As the guitar began to play, I bit my lip and stared at the interior light to hold back my tears.

Simon adjusted his rear-view mirror so that he could see me.

'You okay? Are you sad?'

'No,' I replied, cracking at the seams, 'I'm just really … really happy.'

We spent the rest of the drive in complete and total silence. Rewinding the film and thinking about tomorrow.

Break over. The bell was about to go. Get in line, two by two.

Silence, please.

Silence, I said!

We dropped Lola off at Porte d'Orléans and Simon drove me home and stopped right outside my door.

Just as he was about to pull away I put my hand on his arm: 'Wait here, it'll only take a minute.'

I rushed over to Monsieur Rashid's.

'Here,' I said, handing him the packet of rice, 'don't forget your shopping now.'

He smiled.

He kept his arm raised for a long time, then once he had turned the corner I went back over to my favourite grocer's and bought some dog biscuits, and a tin of dog food.

'Garance, I warning you, your dog piss one more time on my aubergines, I gonna wax him too!'